BENEATH THE BLUEBONNETS

TALES OF TERROR BY TEXAS WOMEN

EDITED BY CARMEN GRAY

CASTLE BRIDGE MEDIA
DENVER, COLORADO, USA

CASTLE BRIDGE MEDIA
Denver, Colorado

Cover art by Joyce Hankins/Unsplash, Benaoquan/Unsplash, Wolfgang Hasselmann/Unsplash. These images have been modified.

This book is a work of fiction. Names, characters, business, events, and incidents are the products of the authors' imaginations. Any resemblance to actual persons, living or dead or actual events is purely coincidental.

BENEATH THE BLUEBONNETS:
TALES OF TERROR BY TEXAS WOMEN
2026© Castle Bridge Media and Individual Authors.
All rights reserved.

ISBN: 979-8-9940410-1-7

TABLE OF CONTENTS

FOREWORD

By Carmen Gray

I ENTERED THE WORLD OF horror writing about ten years ago when E. R. Bills invited me to contribute to the first *Road Kill: Texas Horror by Texas Writers* anthology. I was honored, but I had never written in the genre before. Ideas came and went, none of them quite taking hold, as the deadline crept closer. Could I create something truly worthy? I wasn't sure I could.

At that time, horror wasn't something I had to imagine. It was all around me. My thirteen-year-old daughter had just survived cancer. My marriage had unraveled. I was emerging from a toxic relationship, trying to find my footing again. I could have invented a monster, but instead I chose to write from a place where horror was real and deeply human.

The story I wrote was about human trafficking. Its protagonist was a young girl. It wasn't what the editors expected. About ninety percent of the stories in the collection were written by men, and though they accepted my piece somewhat tentatively, questioning how exactly it qualified as "horror," they ultimately included it. By the narrowest of margins, it found its way in. Only two of the fifteen contributors were women, and I was one of them.

Much to everyone's surprise, a *Fort Worth Star* article later called my story, *Daniel's Dilemma*, the standout piece. It was tragic and unsettling. It was feminine. Atmospheric. And it lingered.

That first publication sent me across Texas for book signings in San Antonio, Austin, Houston, and even a tiny bookstore in Port Aransas, where I met readers I'd never known I had. It opened doors, forged connections, and began a process of healing I hadn't anticipated. Because wounds, I learned, fester when they stay hidden.

Since then, I've written many more short stories, published poetry and magazine articles, a YA tale, and have two fiction novels on their way to being published. But it was the *Femme Fatale* collection in 2021 that reawakened something in me. Published by Jason Henderson and In Churl Yo at Castle Bridge Media and edited by P. J. Hoover, it offered a platform for stories by women, for women. I loved being part of that community of writers, and it was there I met Jess Hagemann, one of the contributors to this collection. The experience planted a seed. I knew I wanted to curate my own anthology, and I knew Castle Bridge would be the one to bring it to life.

From Mary Shelley to Tananarive Due to Mariana Enríquez, women writers of horror have traveled a long and often overlooked road to recognition. Yet women have always lived closest to horror's edge. Forced marriages, lost autonomy, violence, childbirth, survival—these are not distant fears. They are embodied trauma, passed down through generations. Our stories rise from that raw intersection of terror and endurance.

The tales that follow are rooted in Texas, a land both beautiful and savage, steeped in haunted histories and, in recent years, shadowed by laws that seek to diminish women's power. Written by Texas women I've encountered throughout my journey—from *Road Kill* to Castle Bridge, from my Austin literary circle to the Texas Book Festival—this collection gathers diverse voices as varied and vast as the state itself.

Lauren Oertel, whom I met through the Texas Book Festival, helped shape the title, inspired by the idea that something uneasy stirs beneath the bluebonnet-dotted hills of Texas. These writers illuminate the darkness within the collective female imagination, where fear is not merely a literary device. Their stories disturb, provoke, and linger, proving that women's voices in horror are not only essential but among the most arresting in the genre.

Each story in this collection offers its own shade of darkness—some psychological, some supernatural, some rooted in the stark realism of women's lives. Together, they form a mosaic of fear and resilience, revealing that horror is not a single genre but a spectrum.

Be prepared to be haunted, and perhaps to flinch, as you read. I did. May these tales both empower and unsettle you, reminding us that darkness is not only something to fear, but something to face, understand, and ultimately transform. In confronting it, we find not only entertainment, but revelation— and sometimes the beginnings of healing.

Note: The stories in this collection contain mature themes and depictions of violence, trauma, and emotional distress that may be disturbing to some readers.

BETTINA

By R. J. Joseph

MISERY SUBSUMES ALL IT TOUCHES, decay and beauty alike. The rot permeating from the stately home and lush grounds tainted what should have been a sublime spring day. The noise from the horses' shoes on the fertile earth along the roadway could not drown out the misery I heard and felt from that soil. Cries of anguish entreated me to turn around, to leave, to resist becoming trapped as they were. How could I find joy in my heart when my soul cried out with theirs, understanding I would surely meet my end as dreadfully as they, forcefully tethered to one who I despised and, moreover, feared?

There was nothing titillating about the abject terror rising inside me the day I arrived at what was to be my new home—my marriage home. Father had expressly forbidden me to return to my childhood residence, insisting I not bring dishonor upon him and Mother by refusing the agreement he had made with Edward's father that Edward and I were to marry.

Edward was my cousin—but how I hated him! Hated what he had become, although he was once a peculiar child I had played with many times on the same grounds we would live on, growing more trepidatious as time passed and whose mannerisms grew more audacious. The kindhearted child I used to be felt pity towards him and his affliction—monomania—which caused him to fixate on various minute objects and interests the rest of us held in only a passing fancy.

His affliction, I could live with. His cruelty, I would not.

This cruelty was on full display as my carriage approached the big house and he stepped out from behind a row of Black faces and bodies as Black as ours—yet marred by various proofs of Edward's maltreatment of them. The young girl with fresh scars across her face. The old man balanced on his right foot while leaning on a cane that pronounced his missing left foot. The younger woman who flinched as Edward brushed against her in the most brutish of manners. The fear in all pairs of eyes, mirroring that in my own, surely.

He helped me down from my carriage, falsities in place, manufactured charm in full display.

"Bettina. Welcome to our home." I cringed when his cold lips met my gloved hand, the iciness of his demeanor permeating the fine cloth.

I tilted my head in a slight bow as I had been taught since childhood to perform, in deference I did not feel towards him—deference I rarely felt to any other person. "Edward."

I allowed him to lead me towards the servants he had lined up to greet me. He introduced them as a group, in an offhand manner, then attempted to steer me away from them and into the house. I resisted and went to each person, individually, introducing myself and asking their names, offering each the same bow of deference I had been forced to provide Edward, this time the gesture genuine on my part.

My heart constricted as, one by one, their eyes opened in wonderment at my insistence on offering my hand, as well. Not one of them took it. I gave them warm smiles, despite their reticence, determined to show them with my treatment of them that I was not at all the same monster as my husband-to-be had proven himself.

His monstrosity was no secret in our family. At one point, the adolescent Edward became deadly focused on human appendages. One by one, he severed the hands, feet, arms, and legs from various slaves' bodies. More than one female slave had at least one breast viciously removed in his onslaught. Poor old John, who I had greeted in the yard upon my arrival, had been one of his victims.

My favorite old cat in his home, Penny, had also been victimized by him. He cruelly forced her from me one afternoon and spent the evening severing her limbs from her body, one by one—bit by bit. Her screams of anguish permeated even the thick draperies in the house, where I had hidden, inconsolable and unable to rescue her.

The only reason Father finally gave in to my ceaseless begging to never go play at Edward's again after that was because his last fixation devastated his family's inventory of slaves; not because his violence towards other living beings had been acknowledged or rectified.

He had moved on from that fixation, I supposed. However, one never knew when he might return to it—or develop a nastier one.

At dinner on my arrival night, Edward droned on and on about how fruitful he had made his father's plantation. My spirit wept at the pride beaming from him at his descriptions of forced mating between slaves to increase inventory and brutal, long hours of field work for them, with reduced food rations to save money for other investments.

Father also spoke of our slave-owning kin with the same pride. I had always been appalled at the sin in holding others in bondage against their will, especially since we were also Black people.

How was any of that brutality and objectification justified? How could I be proud of a family legacy built on such abominable cruelty? How could I be expected to carry out the bloody legacy of enslavement through birthing children I did not want to bear in the first place?

I had not much choice but to agree to the arrangements my father had made for my adulthood security, whether I agreed with them or not. I could, however, decide I would never bear children within that union. I could also use my new circumstances to do as much as I could to improve the lives of the enslaved in my proximity. Edward had a copious inheritance. As his wife, I would have some access to those funds. Freedom for slaves required funding and I was willing to do what I must to gain those funds. As a concession, Edward was the devil I already knew well.

I feigned a headache and retired to my bed early on that first night, racing up the old wooden staircase with Lita, the young woman Edward had "gifted" me with to be my servant, following quickly behind me. I beseeched her to sit while I undressed myself, accepting her assistance only when she adamantly refused to rest. I noticed her hesitance to leave my room and recognized the return of her fear. I was certain she could feel the same emanating from me.

I made the decision to allow her to sleep in my room with me and helped her find a cot to make up for her sleep. I could not trust Edward to hold to the promise to not visit my bed until after we were married and as long as he did abide by it, Lita was in danger from him if she slept in the slave quarters. We both fell into troubled sleep, made only slightly less tumultuous by the relative safety we afforded one another against our common enemy.

Edward was fiercely unhappy at my actions and did not attempt to hide his feelings the next morning. The long, furtive glares he sent my way unnerved me as he performed them in utter silence. I felt his gaze burn through my bosom and settle in my womb, twisting and pinching the flesh found there until I grew increasingly more uncomfortable. Perhaps he sought to punish me through these visual assaults—I do not know. I worked harder to forget the ways he stared through me.

This task was next to impossible. Around every corner and through every window, his cruel gaze appeared, dissecting me. Part of me wanted to know his accompanying thoughts. The other part wisely tried to ignore him completely. To my surprise, he did not attempt to engage me in conversation after that first night and I took my dinners alone or with Mary and Lita. Nor did he do anything against the major change I had made to Lita's sleeping arrangements. Instead, he seemed preoccupied with a foreign matter. His distraction emboldened me to make several more changes to the way he had previously mis-managed the house.

I asked old John to take on the much gentler task of overseeing the stable boys, instead of him doing the same work they did, a position he could perform while sitting in the large chair Lita and I dragged outside for him to sit in. I asked Mary to allow me to help her in the kitchen sometimes so I could learn to cook. I gave little Charlotte the task of learning to read the storybooks I had packed along with me so I could take on her duties in the kitchen. I also arranged for a stipend from my own household allotment—which Edward had wordlessly assigned—to pay each one of them, with Charlotte's going inside her hidden piggy bank, for the jobs they performed. I had not ended slavery. I had not even emancipated the slaves in my own home. I had not begun to work on improving the plight of the field workers. Yet, I felt much better about having changed what I could inside the house as a first step.

My new duties kept me busy for long days. Once I realized I had not seen Edward much during that time, unease rose inside me. Wearing a better dress than I had taken to wearing around the house of late—in case feminine cajoling or distraction was necessary to assuage whatever further ire I might incite in him—I sought him out. His gazes at me seemed to indicate lustful frustration and while I did not wish to further inflame those thoughts, I also understood I had to play my role as that of willing bride-to-be.

I did not welcome even the thought of having him in my bed, though I knew it was part of my responsibility of being his wife. We were not yet married, however, so I would keep him at an arm's length while he could at least gaze upon my visage, which he apparently found attractive. Such machinations might prove useful in requesting an increased household allotment so I could pay more of people taking care of our property. Still, my goal was not to elevate his lust any higher than my goal required. I was still learning about contraception for when I could no longer hold off his sexual advances. I would not have any children, no matter how often he came to me. It was difficult to remember exactly when I decided not to be bred like some animal, forced to bear and suckle young I did not need or want. I enjoyed children well enough—I simply did not want to bear any of my own. I knew better than to voice this objection to anyone, especially my parents, who both would have died in apoplectic fits at hearing me deny them of what they deemed their God given right to be grandparents and have their familial line continued through me.

Edward had discussed our future children at length for the duration of when he and Father made the arrangements for our union. I pretended to not hear the surreptitious tone raised in his voice at those times. He wanted babes desperately—I was just as desperate to not give them. I had a higher purpose I was dedicated to achieving and birthing children was not a part of that purpose.

My search for Edward took me across the expanse of the plantation. The lush soil yielded underneath my slippers and each step I took came with renewed hopelessness and desolation emanating from the ground bathed in the blood of other Black brothers and sisters who had lived and died horribly on that land. I breathed in the spring air, seeking relief—yet it was tainted by the smell of sweat and despair of those enslaved on Edward's property. I sought to make the air truly light one day by ridding us all of the plague that was slavery.

I finally came to a cabin at the edge of the plantation. Curiosity drew me into it, as I had not ventured that far on the grounds since my return as an adult. The cabin had not been there when I had visited as a child. The light from the open door fell upon a sketched form lying on the floor. My eyes adjusting to the dim light flowing into the room revealed more sketches in various positions. I located a candle and lit it so I could further my investigation.

I do so wish I had not given in to that infernal, insatiable inquisitiveness.

Before me, in various stages of completion were dozens—nay, hundreds— of grotesque sketches, which evoked in me feelings of sickness and dread. Violent swirls of black and red marked canvas, after canvas, designed in ways I did not immediately understand—even as they frightened me immensely. One complete drawing of a female form cast an insidious light on the other works and I grew faint in my realization. On it were highlighted the womb and the breasts, both shown with jagged slashes marring the shapes.

The candlelight caught clay forms and bathed their surreal details in eerie revelation. Large forms shaped as wombs, small forms shaped as pairs of breasts, all serrated around the edges as if savagely torn from the bodies to which they belonged. I then comprehended the incomplete drawings for what they were—shredded pieces from the whole of those body parts. Other works depicted babes in wombs, clawing their way out—babes chewing at the bloodied breasts that suckled them. The strange glances and stares I had grossly misinterpreted as lust became clear in that dusty cabin filled with the monstrous artwork: Edward had found a new focus for his monomania.

I fled the cabin and ran the entire way back to the main house, followed by haunted whispers grown into audible moans and admonitions for me to save myself, lest I be yet another victim fallen into bondage.

I gathered Lita, Mary, and old John together to tell them about my macabre discovery. I did not delude myself that I had earned their complete trust in the short time I had been there—however, I beseeched them to help me do what I knew needed to be done. Lita's eyes lit up.

Old John praised God. Mary patted my hand and said she would make the first steps.

Later that evening, Edward requested to have dinner with me and arrived at the table in a sweaty, manic state. How had I not noticed how glossy his eyes had grown—? How could I have overlooked the way his body twitched and danced even as he sat? I murmured platitudes when I was able to hold down the bile threatening to spew through my throat. Edward paid no attention to my discomfort. Tension boiled up and up in my chest and I gasped aloud several times when Edward started to speak disjointedly about "our" children. Thankfully, he did not continue long because he fell too drowsy to hold his head up. Mary had, indeed, taken the first steps.

When Edward finally collapsed onto the table, Lita and Mary emerged from the kitchen with a large cloth and old John brought four stable boys into the dining room to help us drag Edward onto the bed sheet. Moving quickly through the night, a forbidden band of ghosts travelling through the sighs and whispers of older ghosts, we arrived at the defiled cabin. Old John had spent the afternoon setting up a different type of artistic space for our endeavors. We lay Edward on the floor, fastening the shackles that were built into the floor of the cabin. We barely had time to make sure they were tightened before Edward began to wake. His gaze filled with fury as he realized his situation. He began to laugh frenetically, loud maniacal bursts of noise free of humor. Before he could form any words, I grabbed the serrated blade old John had thoughtfully lain out and stabbed at Edwards mouth. In the aftermath of his shock, I forced the blade into his mouth and cut his tongue out in a jagged swipe.

Lita cut his trousers off with another knife and viciously removed his penis with exaggerated motions, leaving uneven ripples of flesh around the gaping wound. Old John sat slowly on the floor next to Edward and relished in slowly and unevenly sawing at his tormentor's foot with a large saw blade. Mary held Edward's leg down to allow the older man his due.

I again wielded the blade I had claimed and removed one of his ears. Spurred on by the hate in his eyes, I removed the other, taking great care to leave irregular cut patterns. Edward passed out after the second one. Mary and Lita and I helped old John remove most of Edward's other leg, to just above the knee. Mary tied off the stump to prevent him from bleeding out. We then went to work on his arms.

When our task was completed, the three of us surveyed our handiwork. The white of the sheet, dark red of his blood, and the black of his skin matched the color scheme of the other oddities—of his creation—in the same room. Blood flowed copiously through the cloths we applied but Edward would remain alive. He would be unable to speak or move around unassisted but he should not expire unless we deemed it so at some later point—a certain event to occur at an undetermined time after I secured the means we all desperately needed from him.

Most importantly, he would not be able to hurt anyone else ever again.

We returned Edward to the house after day or so when we were relatively sure he would not develop an infection—which also happened to be after I severed the nerves in his eyelids and his neck to prevent him from communicating effectively to anyone else. I had likely destroyed more than only those nerves in what was left of his body—no matter, as he only had to remain alive until after our nuptials. I sent a stable boy into town to alert the authorities and doctor that a terrible accident had befallen my betrothed.

He had been found in the woods alongside our property, the apparent victim of a vicious animal attack. Just look at the jagged and frayed edges of flesh that remained! I apologize. I feel extremely faint when I must gaze upon the wounds. I swoon! Yes, it is a pity what happened to him. No, he does not seem able to communicate with anyone except me. He will need lifetime care. I am insulted at the mere hint of the idea that I no longer wish to marry him! We will marry immediately.

Of course, I, his betrothed, will take excellent care of him. I weep for the babes I will not be able to nurture alongside my beloved. Alas, it was not meant to be for our union. I will find my fulfillment in caring for him, alone. No, I do not require any additional help—Edward has left our estate in perfect order and the accounts hold an excess of funds to continue the management of our plantation and household for many years to come.

Edward and I would live together on his family estate until our final days—he, my singular focus—of course, outside my immediate freeing of our slaves and hiring those who were willing to work at fair wages. I, the singular focus of his enduring nightmare with no legacy to pass on other than that of having to watch, silently, as the household progressed without his influence—and never knowing when or how his ultimate and imminent end at my own hand would come.

ROUTINE SURGERY

By Lauren Oertel

AFTER CHECKING IN AT THE front desk, Hannah sinks into the chair in the back corner. It's closest to the door where patients are called back for their turn. She hopes her proximity to it will somehow reduce the amount of time she needs to spend in this place.

She checks the time on her phone and then sees the large clock on the wall across from her. It's two minutes behind. The ticking of seconds mirrors her pulse.

The smells of sweat and milk overpower the traditional antiseptic scents expected for medical spaces, making Hannah queasy. One woman squirms in her chair, wringing her hands in stress. A teenager with acne-pocked cheeks holds her protruding belly while her eyes flicker back and forth across the waiting room. Another woman rocks her crying baby, begging for the wails to stop.

Hannah massages the back of her neck, where a knot has developed. She assesses the other patients, guessing what brought them to this OB/GYN waiting room in Austin. The clock ticks louder, her pulse rate keeping up with the pace.

Some patients are there because those pink lines appeared when they weren't wanted. Hannah didn't envy their fear. Things were changing faster than any clock could keep up with. The teenager with puffy eyes in the other corner might need to drive out of state, likely to Hannah's home state of New Mexico.

Ten patients in the room already have kids—a baby flailing in a stroller, a toddler climbing on the chairs in a rage about the lack of entertainment, and a few that are suspiciously quiet. The mothers wear their exhaustion in their spit-up-stained shirts and greasy hair that just needs to stay out of the way.

An older woman in orthopedic shoes bounces a toddler on her knees while the younger woman leaning toward them in a slump in the seat next to her has vacant eyes. The boy has a dinosaur Band-Aid on his forehead. It's upside down, and Hannah has the urge to reapply it right side up.

While the posters on the walls show happy families glowing in the love and joy of having their healthy babies, Hannah knows that along with those desperate to end their pregnancy, some want to be pregnant. They dream of the life depicted in those images. They crave the chaos of parenting, but they are "high risk" and know the new laws prevent doctors from doing what is necessary in the worst-case scenarios. They want their babies but they also want to stay alive to raise them.

The clock's ticks grow even louder, and the time it shows is now three minutes ahead of the time on her phone. The idea of time speeding up drifts into thoughts of Dan. The anger returns. How could he have changed his mind so easily? How could he ruin what they had after she left everything she knew in Albuquerque to start a new life with him in Austin?

It had been a slow betrayal.

Dan was the third relationship that ended because of "the kid question." Hannah knew to bring it up early to prevent wasted time for either of them.

"I haven't thought about it too much, but I don't think I have the energy for kids. They're a lot of work and money, aren't they? Sorry. You want kids?" he had said over their second-date tacos when Hannah asked the big question.

She had laughed. "No! What a relief. Should we get another round of beer and cheers to no kids?" His response meant there was potential for a third date.

A few years and many dates later, they had packed up their lives in New Mexico. They said goodbye to their families and drove east to start fresh in Austin. It was for Dan's career, but he promised Hannah she'd find a job quickly since there would be more opportunities there compared to Albuquerque.

It hadn't been easy, but after a few months and dozens of interviews, Hannah settled into a customer service office job that was only moderately soul-sucking.

The crash of a sippy cup hitting the floor jolts Hannah back into the present moment. The child starts to cry as their mother scrambles with wipes to clean up the spill. She mumbles apologies to everyone, but most had quickly forgotten the incident and returned to the screens in their hands.

"Hannah? The doctor is ready for you," an assistant calls from the door.

She springs from her chair and follows the assistant to enter the hallway of exam rooms, entering into room number five.

After twenty minutes of waiting on a pleather couch, Hannah hates the feeling of sitting on the crinkly paper of the exam table. The doctor finally enters, introducing herself with an ice-cold outstretched hand. She is Dr. Anita Clark.

"You're here to discuss a permanent option for birth control?" She flips through the chart in her hands, seeking more information she was unlikely to find there.

"Yes. I'm thinking a tubal ligation makes the most sense."

"Okay, and why do you want this procedure?"

Hannah frowns. Was it a trick question? "To prevent…pregnancy?"

"You're not sure?"

"No, I'm definitely sure I want to prevent pregnancy. Forever. I mean, permanently."

"So you're not pregnant now?" Dr. Clark checks her chart again to see if that had been missed before.

"No, I'm not."

A poster with fine-print disclaimers hangs on the wall in front of Hannah. It's slightly crooked, and there's a faint square of discoloration around it, like it's a recent replacement of a larger poster. She squints to read it, but the doctor continues her line of questioning.

"And you're 100% sure you never want to be? You don't think you'll change your mind?" The doctor notes that Hannah being in her early 30s still provides some time to go in the other direction.

A bead of sweat slides down Hannah's spine. She glares at the wall, trying to keep her nerves in check, but the other posters of fetuses and pregnant bellies make her shiver and refocus on the floor.

No, she won't change her mind like Dan had, and then tried to convince her to do the same. He said it was his parents pressuring him for grandkids since he was an only child, but then he started going down internet rabbit holes of funny baby videos and little league coaching. Hannah could tell she had lost both him and their plans together.

She needed to avoid getting in the same situation again. Future dates would have "the kids question" turned into a statement. She would not have them and her body would no longer have the capability. She would be less vulnerable to that pressure.

"Hannah? I asked if you are 100% sure," the doctor says impatiently, snapping her out of her thinking.

"Sorry. Yes. I am 100% sure."

"And you don't have a husband?"

"No, I don't." Hannah clenches her jaw at the question.

The doctor continues for a few minutes about potential future husbands and their needs but Hannah maintains her position and makes it clear that this is her decision.

The doctor sighs, then explains that a new law requires Hannah to return for a future appointment to view a mandated video before they can schedule the procedure. "Then we can get this taken care of, okay?" The doctor's eyes sit atop puffy skin, showing exhaustion.

Hannah doesn't like the sound of a "mandated video," but agrees to schedule the additional appointment because there isn't another choice.

#   #   #

Two weeks later, the waiting room is even busier than her first visit. Hannah, surrounded by babies and pregnancy, begins panicking as if it could all be contagious.

The clock on the wall across from her ticks so loudly she can hear it over the cries of the babies in the room. This time, it's five minutes fast.

Hannah pleads for the assistant to call her back soon and get her out of the waiting room. She also needs to return to work as soon as possible since they haven't loved her requests for time off for the appointments. And she hasn't even requested the week off for the surgery recovery yet.

In the exam room, Dr. Clark greets Hannah after a twenty-five-minute wait, looking even more overworked than the previous visit. The hair at her temples sticks to her skin with a thin film of sweat.

"Hello again. Sorry about this, but legally, you have to watch this and I have to stay in the room to ensure you're watching it." Dr. Clark starts the video on the screen above the cabinets.

The video includes a montage of happy families paraded in front of viewers and brief interviews with women about how much their kids are everything and how they never knew true love until they gave birth. The Texas Governor closes out the video by explaining that raising children is the most beautiful thing a woman can do. According to him, the alternative is a painful existence, especially for those who choose to prevent the miracle of life from happening in their bodies. Black and white images of lonely women crying fill the screen before Dr. Clark turns off the video.

Hannah gapes at the doctor with an *Are you kidding me?* look.

The doctor chews her lip and apologizes. She glances at the door before sharing that she has to show the video to anyone who requests birth control now, even just the pills.

Hannah also looks at the door and tries not to think about all those teenagers and young adults out there who are in line for brainwashing.

"Do you still want to move forward with the procedure?"

"Yes, as soon as possible." Hannah grabs her purse and fights the urge to run to the scheduling desk down the hall.

The soonest appointment available is five weeks out. After leaving the doctor's office, the time pressure haunts Hannah everywhere she goes. The TV in the breakroom at work always has the news on and the screen reminds her that the Texas state legislature is in session. Those people in suits are debating more restrictions on reproductive health.

She didn't think things could go further than the abortion ban, but that propaganda video she watched proved the government was pushing well beyond that.

The radio blares with more details on the debates on her drive home from the office, and she smashes the power button with her thumb to replace those terrifying words with silence. Since when did restaurants and coffee shops need to play the news too? It seemed to create more confusion than clarity and everyone seemed to become more frazzled with the overwhelm of trying to follow it.

In her studio apartment, she calls her parents, who encourage her to move back home, but she is determined to make it work. As long as she has the surgery, she can move on with her life in Austin and rebuild her life again after Dan.

She hopes to meet someone new and let go of the worries of accidents or persuasion. There had to be decent men in Austin who shared her desire to live a kid-free life. But until the surgery happened, she avoided any risks. No dating apps or even friendly conversations that could lead to something romantic.

On the day of the surgery, Hannah exits the rideshare car and struggles to avoid asking the friendly woman in the driver's seat if she could stay with her for the day. She had hoped her friend Jess would be able to take her, but Jess had a work trip out of state so Hannah was on her own. There were prepared meals to just reheat and carry herself through her recovery and besides, Dr. Clark had said it would be minimal recovery time.

Nearly all of Hannah's connections in Austin were lost in the breakup with Dan, so Jess is her emergency contact. She promised to visit Hannah as soon as she was back in town. She was also from Albuquerque, and while they hadn't known each other growing up there, they bonded quickly once Hannah saw Jess flash a New Mexico ID to enter The White Horse one night during her first week in Austin.

Hannah hadn't felt comfortable telling her boss or colleagues what her surgery was for, so she just told everyone she'd be out for a week "for a medical procedure," and they didn't pry. A few wished her good luck, but her job wasn't exactly an environment for making close friends.

In the surgery center's waiting room, which is much smaller than the OB/GYN office's, Hannah fills out the forms and hopes they won't have an emergency since her parents and Jess are many miles away. Another large and loud clock on the wall ticks away time at a glacial pace. What was with these places and their clocks?

After filling out what felt like hundreds of forms and signing numerous times that she understands the risks, etc., Hannah is handed a gown and a nurse begins an IV in her arm. The quick shift from waiting and everything moving slowly to the rush of preparing for surgery makes her head spin. Where is Dr. Clark?

As soon as the anesthesiologist attaches a tube to Hannah's arm, the brain fog creeps in, and her veins feel like Icy Hot is running through them.

An older man with a thick white beard appears before her and introduces himself as Dr. Stevens.

"Dr. Clark had something come up, so I'm stepping in for your procedure today."

Hannah tries to respond, but her words melt together. A nurse forces her to concentrate on holding a pen so she can sign one final consent form. She uses the remainder of her energy to scribble a shape resembling her signature. The room and everyone around her fade into a hazy space of nothingness.

Hannah wakes in the smaller room where she first changed into the gown. The curtain in front of her screeches open, and Dr. Stevens approaches her.

"Everything went well. I expect you to have a smooth recovery."

"Sorry, who are you?" He looks familiar, but everything from the past few hours is a blur.

He laughs in an overly jolly way. "Oh, you were a bit out of it earlier, but I told you I am Dr. Stevens."

Hannah's eyes widen. "Did something happen to Dr. Clark?"

"No, she had a patient emergency. Anyway, here are your instructions for recovery, and I think you should be back to normal after a week or two. Maybe even back out on the dating scene." He lifts an eyebrow and grins.

Hannah recoils, and her stomach turns. The sourness of the painkillers wearing off, mixed with the confusion of coming out of the anesthesia, makes her hand fly to her mouth.

"That's normal. Don't worry about any vomiting today. The nausea is the toughest part of the recovery process. I'll let the nurse take it from here. You can get dressed and get some rest at home now."

Hannah nods and grabs the bag the nurse hands her just in time to puke into it.

#   #   #

The rideshare drive home feels endless. Hannah begs her stomach to hold up through the turns and bumps and keeps her eyes closed to avoid more motion sickness. The male driver is likely annoyed by the passenger he is stuck with, but Hannah focuses on just making it to her doorstep. When her key hits the lock, she retches on her front door.

Welcome home, she thinks, heading for the couch as she lowers herself onto it, relieved to drift into sleep again. A few days later, Jess stops by with some new meals and a generous offer to do some laundry. Hannah is grateful for the help but mainly wants someone to talk with after everything.

"It's almost weird how smoothly it's gone after the surgery day. I got sick from the anesthesia and painkillers they gave me in the IV, but once I was past that part, it's been fine."

"Well, that's good, right? Do you have stitches?" Jess asks.

"I think only on the inside. I just have these tiny lines with tape on my stomach, and they seem to be healing quickly." Hannah points to the incision marks and then lowers her shirt back down.

"Well, I'm glad you got it over with, and I might want to do the same soon. I haven't been able to keep up with the news during my work trip, but I've heard they're doing ridiculous things here. The two kids I already have are plenty."

"Yeah, I'm avoiding all news since I don't need the stress. I'm sure I'll be bombarded with it again on Monday when I'm back at work."

Hannah asks Jess for details about her Denver trip since she wants to take her mind off politics and surgery. They catch up on other things and joke about what they miss the most and least from Albuquerque. They miss enchiladas "Christmas" style with both red and green chili sauce. They don't miss those terrible goat head stickers that could attach themselves to socks or find their way into a sandal.

"I have been stabbed enough by those to last a lifetime," Jess says.

"Seriously. And while the government here seems to be crazy, at least we don't have to reapply lotion every hour since there's moisture in the air here, right?" Hannah says, convincing herself that she's in a better place. "My job does pay more here," she adds.

"True and there's plenty to love here. Just stay away from the news." Jess yawns and heads for the door. "I can hear my kids yelling about dinner from here." After opening the door, she offers to give the puke spot a second clean.

"Ugh, how embarrassing. Sorry you had to see that—"

"More like I smelled it." Jess pinches her nose but then laughs. "Want help?"

"It's fine, I got it. I feel pretty much back to normal." Hannah grabs a cleaning towel and a spray bottle of cleaner. She pulls over a small stool to sit on and starts scrubbing.

Hannah's return to work goes better than expected. Mainly because someone had finally changed the channel on the TV in the breakroom, and no one bothers her with prying questions about her surgery. She finds new energy to get through each workday and starts to look for a new hobby to take on and new people to meet. Maybe standup paddle boarding, or Skee-Ball, or sand volleyball at one of the bar courts downtown. It feels like she's finally turning a corner.

But things start to change a few weeks later. The breakfast tacos she makes every morning start to taste rotten. Even oatmeal sets her stomach on edge.

After lunch at the office, Hannah is on a call with an especially unhappy customer. Her stomach sours, and she hits mute just in time to make it to the trash can.

She slumps in her chair while the customer drones on about their dissatisfaction. Once she gets through it, she ties the trash can liner then grabs her purse and keys and rushes to her car to get home. The trash bag plops into a dumpster with a soft thud. Her mind spins during the drive—did something go wrong in the surgery? Should she call the doctor's office first, or the surgery center? Or was it food poisoning?

On her way out of the office, she texts Jess about what's been happening.

As soon as she pulls out of the parking lot, Jess calls. "Something is not right. Have you seen the latest?"

"News? No, it actually hasn't been on at work for some reason. It's been a relief."

"Can you hear this?" Jess turns up the volume on the TV blaring the news at her house.

Hannah hears a reporter explain, "In an unprecedented turn of events, really, this should not have been legal; the Texas Governor had expedited the timeline…" Hannah keeps driving toward her apartment, still queasy.

"I'm sorry even to suggest this, Hannah, but I think you need to pick something up on your way home," Jess says.

Before Hannah turns down her street, she pulls into the nearest CVS. Her body buzzes with nausea and fear as she wanders the aisles and then pays for something she never imagined she would have to purchase after her surgery.

In her bathroom, two pink lines make her stumble back into the wall. She slides to the floor and crumbles into herself.

After an hour of sitting with the shock of it, the rage kicks in. She pushes herself up and searches frantically for the documents from her surgery day. She hadn't thought to review them since the recovery had been so smooth.

Scrambling through the paperwork, she hisses with the sting of a paper cut in her panicked search for how things could have gone so wrong.

And then she finds it. The consent form with her anesthesia-hazed signature at the bottom of the last page. All she can see is the word "insemination." The room fades. Her mind shuts down, just like the day of the surgery.

Hannah comes to on the floor, hoping the nightmare has ended. The consent form next to her tells her she isn't so lucky. Grabbing her phone, she texts Jess with the test results, still in shock. Jess sends her numerous cursing face emojis and links to a few articles. The headlines read, "Texas Governor's Executive Order to Ban All Forms of Contraceptives" and "TX

Gov Speeds Up Legislative Process, New Law Effective Immediately." The articles were from six weeks ago, the week of her surgery.

Hannah's shaking finger can barely function when dialing the doctor's office. A receptionist places her on hold. She paces for twenty minutes through the elevator music intended to distract her from how long she is kept waiting.

A glint of silver on the cutting board in the kitchen nook catches her eye. She sets down the phone, with the music continuing to play through the speaker.

TO CIMARRON CITY AND POINTS BEYOND

By L.H. Phillips

"ALL OFF FOR TOMBSTONE!" LILY yelled and pumped the porch swing higher. "Next stop, Dodge City!" The chains on the swing creaked in protest.

"Lily, don't swing so high." Lily's grandmother came out on the porch, a cold Coke in one hand and a napkin folded over two sugar cookies in the other. "I brought you a snack. You sure you don't want to come in and watch my afternoon stories with me?"

"No, ma'am," Lily muttered, taking the offered Coke and cookies. She had been left behind with her grandma this hot July day by, well, *everybody*. Her big sister had gone with her friends to the public swimming pool in their little East Texas town, and had declined to be burdened with eight-year old Lily. Her brother was gone too, helping their granddad on a house painting job. Lily's parents were the only ones with a real excuse in her eyes, since they obviously had to work on a weekday.

"Alright little monkey, stay on the porch or in the backyard, and quit swinging so high.

Someday those chains are going to break with you kids." Lily's grandmother retreated into the relative cool of the living room to watch her soap operas and rest from cleaning up after lunch.

Lily ate the excellent homemade cookies and sulked, bitter as only a young child can be.

It was not fair at all. Margaret had called her a baby when she had begged to go with her to the pool, like being fifteen made her and her friends so superior. Her twelve-year-old brother Paul was still a willing playmate, but he was saving up to buy a guitar and the lure of being paid for helping Grandpa was too great. There was nothing, *nothing* to do this scorching day. Even the kittens her Grandma's cat had given birth to in June were all sleeping in the cool dirt beneath the porch.

Lily had been trying to amuse herself by playing Stagecoach, a game of Margaret's invention, but it was a stupid game for only one person. The whole point was for the driver of the stagecoach (that is, the porch swing) to make it as difficult as possible for the passengers to board or leave the stagecoach by pumping the swing as high as they could.

When the driver yelled out your destination–Tombstone, Dodge City, or farthest out, Cimarron City–you had to bail out of the swing and go stand by one of the porch columns, the columns being discreetly labeled in pencil with the different towns. Likewise, to re-board for a new destination, you had to try and get on the swing as it was arcing wildly between the porch floor and ceiling. It was not an approved game in the grownups' eyes, but

Lily and her siblings loved it. With no one to play with this afternoon, Lily could only shout out town names to imaginary riders, or bail out herself, effectively ending the game. Boring.

Lily finished her soda, finally tiring of her self-pity. An idea came to her, probably a bad one, but totally in tune with her restless mood. She could sneak off and go down to the canyon.

The canyon was a place of glamorous mystery to Lily. Her grandparents owned half an acre beyond the backyard proper that her granddad kept planted in a vegetable garden. Corn, beans, tomatoes and bell peppers all flourished in tidy rows. Beyond the garden were open fields of uncertain ownership filled with dewberry brambles, full of juicy, purple berries in the spring. All of this was very familiar to Lily, but somewhere farther out, where Lily had never been permitted to go, was the canyon. Her brother and sister had been there, and filled Lily with tales of what went on in its walls: A suspicious vagrant was camping in it. A wild horse was spotted galloping in its bottom. College kids went down there in a group and did…Margaret and Paul weren't sure what. And so on. Lily had always been considered too young to go on any of these exploratory missions.

Lily peeked into the living room. Her grandma was dead asleep, tired out from the heat of the day. Lily had been quite clearly told not to leave the immediate vicinity of the house.

She was not usually disobedient or adventurous, but she had worked herself up into a state of aggrieved defiance. She would go to the canyon and see some amazing sight. Later, after supper, she would nonchalantly mention it to Margaret and Paul, and they would be impressed and jealous they had missed it.

Lily walked through the backyard, past the mustang grape vines that divided it from the vegetable garden, past the rustling corn stalks drying in the July sun, and out into the no- man's land of the unused fields. She went carefully, as the fields were full of thorny vines and bull nettles that would punish an unwary walker. The afternoon sun was stupefyingly hot and the weeds buzzed with little red and black grasshoppers.

Lily turned and looked back at her grandparents' white frame house. There were more cold Cokes in the refrigerator in that kitchen. She almost abandoned her plan, but a certain angry stubbornness drove her on. Lily wasn't sure exactly how much farther the canyon was. There was a line of chinaberry trees in the distance, and she made a bargain with herself that she would keep walking at least until she reached that landmark.

By the time she made it to the little group of trees, she was more than ready to stand in their shade and catch her breath. The error of not bringing any water with her had been driven home exceedingly well. She was hot and itchy, but moving a little past the trees, she suddenly forgot all about that. Before her was what must be the legendary canyon. It was really just a large, steep ravine with rocks and sad, scrubby little bushes going down to a sandy bottom. It was deeper and wider than the highway cuts running through the surrounding East Texas hills, but just as ordinary.

Lily was happy to have made it to her goal, but couldn't deny her sense of disappointment. The "canyon" was a glorified ditch. Neither mysterious wanderers nor mystical horses were apparent in it. Not even a stray college freshman. There was a flat rock in the shade of the trees at the edge of the incline, and she sat down on it to rest.

Lily pushed her sweaty bangs out of her eyes and thought about the stories her brother and sister had told her. Were they even true? Lily was the kind of kid who looked at the treetops peeking over a neighbor's house and imagined they were fairy-tale mountains rising in the distance. She had thought her older siblings led less boring lives than she, and didn't need to imagine places of enchantment and romance the way she did. Maybe she was wrong.

Lily stood up, debating whether to head back to the house right away or wait a while and see if anything happened. She felt uneasy all of a sudden, without being sure why. The afternoon had gone completely silent. The background hum of the grasshoppers was gone; no birds rustled and twittered in the trees. The air, already oppressively hot, seemed to press down on her with an actual weight as if she were trapped beneath an immense, smothering beast. Gasping a little, Lily looked down into the gully.

Some kind of distortion in the air was occurring down there, like heat waves coming off of asphalt. At the center of the distortion, Lily saw what appeared to be a large slab of granite. Had that been there before? She leaned forward and rubbed her eyes to try to remedy the odd blurriness. Was it actually rectangular? She couldn't understand how she could have missed seeing it before. It looked at least six feet long and maybe four feet wide.

The thing was somehow elevated above the sandy ground, although Lily's eyes kept refusing to focus on it properly. A dull pounding started at the base of her skull.

The harder she stared at it, the harder it seemed to make out any details. Almost without thinking, Lily started picking her way down the slope. Her tennis shoes slipped on the crumbly ground. Once she ended up on her rear end, skinning both hands as she caught herself from sliding all the way down. She was too engrossed to notice. She could hardly take her eyes off of the stone. She needed to get to it and see it properly and relieve the strange anxiety she felt about its exact nature. Probably just a make-shift picnic table or something, Lily told herself.

Lily finally reached the bottom of the gully, accompanied by a small cloud of dust. She approached the slab slowly. It was ancient looking, gray and weathered as an old tombstone.

Here and there on its surface were faint grooves forming swirls and angles whose pattern seem to subtly shift every time Lily glanced away.

Lily bent and looked underneath it and circled all around, hunched over like a pale little crab. There were no supporting columns or legs. The thing was floating. Lily laughed in amazement. She was seeing something impossible. Lily walked around it again to make sure she wasn't mistaken. She started to pass her hand beneath it, like a magician demonstrating a trick, but a sharp pang of fear stopped her. She backed away and watched it with a sudden wariness, as if the stone was a rabid animal that might attack.

"This is dumb," Lily muttered to herself. "It's just a rock." *Yeah,* a deeply concerned inner voice replied, *a rock that's floating in the field behind my Grandma's house.*

"Right," Lily said with a giggle, and then was further unnerved by how loony she sounded.

Lily crept up close to the slab again and reached out a shaky hand. She expected the stone to be hot—it was situated in direct sunlight—but a numbing cold shot through her fingers and up her arm as soon as her fingertips brushed its gray surface. The world around her seemed to blink out and Lily was thrown back several feet as though hit by a cresting wave.

She landed with her butt in the sand and a growing panic in her mind. The world re-asserted itself, but weakly, like a bad TV transmission.

She turned and scrambled up the side of the gully on her hands and knees, oblivious to the damage to her palms and kneecaps. She grabbed a straggly bush at the top of the incline and hauled herself completely out of the gully. Lily hardly paused to catch her breath but started across the field in a staggering run.

Chaotic images flashed through her mind, defying description and leaving her disoriented. She wasn't sure if she was really headed back to the house at all. There weren't supposed to be any buildings in the fields she had crossed to the canyon, but now there was some kind of broken down barn off to her right. Lily paused in confusion to look at this problematic structure. The barn, or whatever it was, was black with age. Its walls and roof did not seem to meet at quite the proper angle, and as Lily watched, the walls folded in and then heaved out as if the building were breathing.

Lily fell to her skinned knees and retched violently, her vision graying out at this insult to reality. After a moment, her stomach settled and she cautiously looked up, wiping tears from her clammy face. To her immense relief, the heaving barn was gone. The only building she could see was her grandparents' white frame house in the distance.

"Don't go away, don't go away," Lily chanted, and began shakily traversing the field again. She stared fixedly at the distant house, afraid it might vanish or turn into something else. When she stumbled into a dewberry bramble (and the red wasp nest concealed within it), it took her a few seconds to realize what she had done. The annoyed wasps swarmed over her ankles, buzzing and stinging, and the world snapped back into a painful, sharp focus.

Lily gave a strangled scream and bolted for the house, crossing the remaining distance in record time. She hit the screen door of the kitchen and fell inside, sobbing. The wasps had abandoned her a number of yards back, deeming sufficient punishment had been doled out to the interloper.

Her grandmother and mother came running from the living room. "Oh, Lily, honey!" her mom exclaimed, seeing her red, swollen ankles and scratched up legs and hands. They sat her down at the kitchen table and put her fiery ankles and feet into a basin of cold water, and began tending to her other scrapes and cuts, wiping her face with a cool washcloth and murmuring consolingly. "Whatever were you doing? Your grandma said you were out back playing with the kittens," her mom said finally, when Lily had calmed down and quit crying.

Lily looked at the kitchen clock. It must be past three o'clock for her mom to already be off work. Sure enough, the clock hands read three-thirty. It didn't seem as though she should have been gone quite that long. Maybe she had stood there gaping at that stupid rock longer than she had thought.

"I was out in the fields a bit, exploring," Lily said. She felt surprisingly secretive about the floating stone. It was her discovery, only for her.

"Didn't your grandma tell you to stay close to the house? You shouldn't have been out there without Margaret or Paul." Lily felt tears starting up again at the mild scolding.

"Ah, never mind, never mind," her mom said. "I guess you'll know not to do it again."

She kissed Lily's forehead, and presently they walked the block home together.

Lily was very quiet that night at supper. She kept pushing her food around her plate with her fork, but it never seemed to achieve an appetizing configuration. Elusive little flashes of light kept playing at the corner of her eye, causing her to jerk her head in their direction, but she could never catch them in full sight. Margaret and Paul paid her more attention than usual—red wasp stings demanded even sibling sympathy—but Lily couldn't muster up much response. She couldn't talk about her experience at the canyon for some reason, or even think about it very coherently. There was such a loud buzzing in her head it seemed the wasps had taken up residence between her ears. At last, her mother exchanged a worried look with her father and picked up her mostly uneaten plate of food.

"Maybe you should go on to bed early tonight, Lily. You'll feel better in the morning."

Lily went without protest, even though her favorite show, *Bonanza*, was on and she would miss seeing her secret crush, Little Joe Cartwright. Lying in the dark of her room was soothing and Lily dropped off to sleep quickly, the muffled sound of the TV in the living room acting as a lullaby.

Sometime later in the night Lily awoke with a start. The house was very still. In her dresser mirror, across from the foot of her bed, she could see a tiny pinpoint of light. As she watched, the pinpoint grew into a luminous, swirling blue cloud. Lily found herself sliding feet first toward this improbable storm like a nail to a magnet. She clutched ineffectually at the bedclothes in an effort to stop her motion. Her feet and legs went off the end of the bed, pulled as straight as a ruler toward the center of the light. Lily grabbed one of the bedposts as her shoulders drew even with it and let out a scream. Her body was pulling painfully toward the mirror, and her fingers were losing their grip on the bedpost. The buzzing in her head was now a roar, the roar a somehow hungry voice that seemed to say *come to me.*

Lily's fingers slipped from the post.

"Lily! What's the matter?" The bedroom light snapped on. Lily found herself on the floor, a parent on either side, helping her sit up.

"She must have rolled out of bed," her dad said.

"Rolled over the footboard? She must really have gotten twisted around," her mother said, and pressed her hand to Lily's forehead. "She's burning up. I think she needs to see Dr. Thomas tomorrow. Maybe she's having a reaction to the wasps." Lily's mother brought her a baby aspirin and tucked her back into bed.

The next day Lily found herself sitting on Dr. Thomas's paper-covered table. Her fever had broken with the morning light but her mom still insisted upon seeing the pediatrician.

He peered at her with his tiny lights and prodded her neck and abdomen.

"I don't see that she is having an allergic reaction of any kind," the doctor said. "Perhaps it was just the emotional upset putting her off kilter. Keep an eye on her the next few days, but I'm sure she'll be fine." He patted Lily's back and gave her a green sucker.

Lily trailed after her mom to the car. The sucker dropped from her fingers in the parking lot. The candy was no more appealing than last night's supper had been.

Lily spent the next few days in a distracted haze. She could barely bear to eat the food put before her, the texture and smell of it being at best bland and at worst repulsive. Everything seemed false, the colors too bright and the sounds too shrill. She had seen beneath the ordinary skin of the world, and now that knowledge was beneath *her* skin, working to change her. She spent more and more of her time sleeping, lost in dreams of dark water and submerged ruins. The incident with the mirror did not repeat itself, and Lily began to feel an anxious regret that whatever had tried to reach her had been interrupted. She was frightened, but there was an unbearable itch in her mind that needed to be soothed, could only be soothed by whatever had been beyond that maelstrom of light. She felt an attraction, an attraction that was almost a command to begin a different existence. Lily wanted to visit the canyon again, but everyone seemed to be watching her very carefully.

A week after Lily had made her trip to the canyon, she awoke no longer anxious and with her thoughts sharply focused for the first time in days.

"Can we go over to Grandma's?" Lily asked Margaret.

"Sure," Margaret said, and exchanged a look with their mother that seemed to communicate a certainty that she would not be left alone.

Lily and Margaret walked the block to the little white house. Grandma fussed over them and gave them ice-pops, even though it was barely nine in the morning.

"I want to swing on the porch some," Lily said. She picked up a pencil from the living room coffee table on her way out.

"Okay," said Margaret. She and Grandma sat down in the living room, positioning themselves so they could watch her through the screen door, Lily noted.

It didn't matter. Lily had had a different sort of dream last night, one that explained exactly what she needed to do.

Lily went to the porch column beyond the one marked "Cimarron City," the one they had decided was a little too far out for the Stagecoach game. She drew a series of triangles and whirls on its base, much like the symbols she had seen on what she now thought of as the stone door. When she was satisfied with the inscription, she threw both the pencil and her ice-pop over into the flower bed.

Lily got into the porch swing. She could see her writing on the column starting to glow.

Lily pumped the swing vigorously. She could hear Margaret and Grandma talking quietly in the house, and she felt a distant sadness she could no longer be with them.

The glow at the end of the porch increased and spread toward the swing, forming a tunnel, a *passageway*. Lily pumped the swing even higher. "R'yleh!" she screamed out, and leapt into the bright and expanding air.

LAST OF THE KILGORE BOOHAGS

By Kathleen Kent

"SEE, THIS HERE'S WHAT YOUR problem is."

The plumber rocks back on his heels and points to the curved elbow of the pipe beneath the kitchen sink.

"There's something clogging up the P trap. Probably a big ole grease ball. You been emptyin' your fat can down the drain again, Mrs. Conroe?"

Donny Conroe gives a bleat of laughter while eyeing his mother's ponderous weight, but does a quick sidestep before she can backhand him. Jerri Dean Conroe looks at the brackish, foul smelling water pooling in the stainless-steel sink and shakes her head doubtfully.

"Why does it smell so bad?" she asks.

To illustrate the point, Donny pinches his nostrils shut with a forefinger and thumb and pulls his mouth down into a grimace. "It stinks," he says. "Smells like a dead cat."

Ellis Hinton has done much of the plumbing fixes in Kilgore for the past fifteen years, and often the common denominator in many of the dwellings in the southerly part of town is a careless indifference to house cleaning. If cleanliness is next to Godliness, then most of the inhabitants of Live Oaks

Trailer Park in south Kilgore are going straight to hell. Surprisingly, for all the jumble of broken toys and car parts in the front yard, the inside of Jerri Dean's trailer doesn't look too bad. Kitchen floor clean, dishes put away, not a lot of empty Frito bags lying around.

"Well, how long has the water been standing?" Ellis asks.

"Just since last night," Jerri Dean answers. "It just sort of leeched up out of the pipes."

Ellis sticks his head beneath the sink again to hide any expressions of disbelief. More like four or five days that water's been standing, he thinks. From the bubbles forming at the surface, it seems as though whatever's in the sink is starting to foster an impressive well of fermenting microbes.

"I'll take the pipe apart, clear out the mess and have you good to go in about ten."

"Okay," she says. "I'll be outside for a bit."

Jerri Dean goes to sit in her lawn chair to smoke. Donny stays for a bit to ask questions. "Ever find any money down in there? What about rings and jewelry and stuff?"–until he gets bored and goes outside to pester his mom.

The only jewelry Donny's ever going to lay claim to in this place, Ellis thinks, will be a plastic decoder ring, unless the retrieved item had been stolen out of some pawnshop.

Ellis had also, on occasion, done plumbing work for the local middle school, as some of the pipes were fifty years old. He'd heard some unsettling rumors from the janitor of Donny Conroe torturing animals too small to bite or claw their way out of his grubby hands. If the bruises on the boy's arms were any clue, the last thing he'd been learning at home was a gentle touch.

It takes him longer than expected to loosen the collar nuts, but as soon as he gets some movement with his wrench, he positions the bucket beneath the trap to catch whatever water will be draining from the sink, as well as from the vertical drain behind the wall.

As soon as the first nut disconnects, the rush of liquid from the sink splashes into the bucket, and Ellis rears back from the stench so quickly that he lands hard on his ass, his hands struggling to find purchase on the linoleum tile. The fluid is viscous, black with clots of solid material that plop into the bucket with a meaty slap. He turns his face away, his eyes watering, while struggling to suppress his gag reflexes. He's unclogged some unholy messes in his time, but never anything this noxious.

What in the Good-God-Almighty has that woman been throwing into her sink?

He must have made a sound of protest because Jerri Dean sticks her head into the trailer and says, "You alright in there?"

She wrinkles her nose at the toxic smell and quickly moves to close the door again.

"Hey," Ellis calls, "can you keep that door propped open? I can't work in here without some clean air."

She props the door open with a laundry basket and moves her chair farther away from the trailer.

Holding a cloth over his nose, Ellis pulls the bucket from under the sink, walks quickly out to the small yard behind the trailer where he dumps the foul mess onto the grass. It glistens in a dark, bubbling stew under the late afternoon sun before seeping into the dirt.

Donny has come to stand next to Ellis, one hand over his mouth and nose, and pointing with the other. He asks in a muffled tone, "What's that?"

Between the thick runners of the Bermuda grass a whole bunch of. . . somethings are squirming. Pale, gelatinous forms–each about as big as a grub worm–are writhing actively around the blades of grass. Donny has picked up a stick and begins to stab at the thrashing worm-like creatures. On close inspection they look to have tiny suckers along one side, and ridged orifices at each end, opening and closing hungrily.

Jerri Dean has come to stand next to Donny, and she pulls him back, away from the things on her lawn.

"What are they? Hookworms?" she asks.

"No, I don't believe they are," Ellis says. "They're too short and fat."

"Mealworms?"

Ellis shakes his head doubtfully.

Before she can stop the boy, Donny has started stomping them with his bare feet.

"Uh, uh, uh," he grunts with each heel strike. "Die, fuckers."

Jerri Dean slaps his head hard with the flat of her palm, knocking him off balance.

"Get in the house right now before I really hit you," she yells.

Donny charges off toward the trailer, and throws himself into the lawn chair, pouting, his arms crossed defensively over his chest.

Jerri Dean's sizeable bulk is blocking the rays of the lowering sun, shadowing the still- writhing patch of grass. "I'm gonna kill that old bitch," she murmurs.

"'Scuse me?" Ellis says.

"That old lady I hired to tend my house. This morning when I told her to clear out the mess in the sink, she told me I was the one causing it, so I had to clean it up myself. I fired her on the spot. I see her again, I'm going to shove her nose into this mess and make her tell me what she did to plug up my Goddamn sink!"

Ellis wonders how in the world Jerri Dean Conroe can afford a cleaning lady, but it does explain the reasonably tidy state of her trailer. She rushes in the direction of the trailer, and returns a minute later with an empty jelly jar. With difficulty she leans over to scoop up some of the worms. When they don't cooperate she uses her finger to prod a few into the jar. One latches on to the tip of her finger, and she squeals as she shakes it into the jar. She then screws the lid on and watches the captured things through the glass, absentmindedly wiping the hand that touched the worms on her pants leg.

"See if the old bitch likes these crawling through her hair," Jerri Dean says triumphantly.

Ellis spends another hour snaking the vertical drain and flushing out the kitchen sink and pipes with bleach. By the time he's packed up his tools the stench in the trailer has been reduced to a near tolerable level. He loses another ten minutes arguing with Jerri Dean about the money he's owed for the work he's done. Nearly an hour and a half to complete a job Jerri Dean thought would be completed in less than half an hour. She finally relents and pays him for the time.

When he gets into his truck to leave, he notices Donny sitting on a rusted tricycle, scratching frantically at one of his bare feet.

The Conroe trailer was his last job of the day, and he calls his boss to let him know he's headed home. After a few miles of narrow farm to market roads he turns north on Route 259. He keeps all the windows in his truck rolled down, but the smell from the trailer seems to cling to his clothes, and the inside of his nostrils, like smoke from a burning cesspit. He wishes he had captured a sample of one of the worm-like creatures in one of Jerri Dean's jelly jars. He would have taken it to his cousin who owned the Yellow Rose Garden Shop, asking her if she'd ever seen, or smelled, anything like it.

The sun is setting to his left, turning the soil a coppery red, the soft afternoon light casting a forgiving mantle over the sparse yards and meager houses fronting the road.

Just before the turn off for the business spur of 259, he spots a woman walking alone on the shoulder of the road. She's walking very slowly, with a limping gate, dragging what appears to be a shopping cart behind her. When he passes her, he sees she's quite old, her face contorted in pain or weariness. He pulls over onto the shoulder, and gets out of the truck.

"Ma'am, you okay?" he calls. "You need help?"

The woman continues her slow and steady progress.

"Your car break down?" he asks.

He walks toward her and sees that, not only is she old, she's positively ancient. Her face is deeply lined, the sections of hair escaping from under her hat are white and wispy as corn silk.

She looks up, her eyes focusing with some difficulty on Ellis, and says, "Haven't got a car."

"Where are you headed?" he asks. "Can I give you a ride?"

"Oh, bless you," she says, patting his arm. She leans in, as though revealing a deep confidence. "I'm going to Longview."

"Ma'am, that's over twelve miles away. Were you thinking you could walk there?"

The woman is not only aged, she's tiny. Less than five feet tall, her back bent, her hands twisted with arthritis.

"Well," she says, looking around as though seeing the downtrodden landscape for the first time. "It's closer than Tyler."

She smiles at him in a self-deprecating and humble way, and he finds he's smiling back at her. She's what his own grandmother would have called True People. Brought low by adversity, but not hardened. Beleaguered by the passage of years, but not embittered. Misshapen by physical trials, but still able to laugh at misfortune.

But it's possible that she's in a state of forgetful dementia. Maybe she'd wandered away from her home and, even now, has family looking for her. As slow as she was moving, she could have walked out of a house only a few hundred yards away.

"You have any people around here?" he asks.

As though reading his thoughts, she says, "There's nothing left for me to do in Kilgore.

But I've got connections in Longview. They'll take care of me."

He gently takes the cart from her with one hand and gives her his other hand to hold on to. Her fingers are dry, the skin as thin as parchment, but the grip surprisingly strong.

They make their way to his truck, and he helps her into the cab after placing her shopping cart in the back. It's filled with plastic bags bulging with what is perhaps the sum total of her belongings.

He gets into the driver's seat and, after making sure she's safely fastened her seatbelt, he continues his drive north.

"I'm Ellis Hinton," he says.

"And I'm Mathilda Belle Johnson. Pleased to meet you."

She holds out her hand to shake his, and he sees with some amusement that the old girl's wearing what looks to be a dozen small bangle bracelets that rattle together pleasantly.

She takes off her hat, and her hair springs free like a gauzy corona around her head, her pink scalp visible beneath the thinning curls. "I have to say, that it feels good to be off my feet."

"Where were you coming from?" he asks.

"From my last job."

He looks at her skeptically, and her smile widens.

"I had a job as a housekeeper. But I got fired this morning." The grin broadens further. She squints her eyes coyly at him, as though the firing was a source of great delight. "The lady of the house had some unwholesome habits, so I was only happy to leave."

He remembers Jerri Dean telling him she'd just fired a housekeeper that morning. "I'm going to kill that old bitch," she had said. But the trailer park was miles away. It didn't seem possible someone this aged and frail could have walked that far. Or even be fit enough to efficiently clean a doublewide trailer. Beyond that, how could a sweet old lady fill a sink with the horrible stinking mess he'd found in the Dean's kitchen? Especially a mess she'd probably have to clean up herself.

And yet. . .the part of his brain that had been working overtime to forget the foul- smelling worms, gives way, and the memory of Donny smashing their glistening bodies with his bare feet, the wet popping sounds as the wiggling forms exploded, fills his head.

The lingering stink seems to swell again inside the cab of the truck, despite the air circulating through the windows, and he cautiously sniffs at his shirt to see if he's the source.

He thinks to ask her the name of the lady who had fired her, but doesn't want to unduly embarrass her. "You live in Kilgore?"

"Until this morning I did."

Her accent is softer, more languorous than East Texas speak.

"Where are you from?" he asks. "I mean, originally?"

"My people were from Charleston, South Carolina. But we moved to New London, just south of here, when I was three years old. We were a big family. I was one of eleven girls. The youngest of ten sisters, with no brothers, if you can imagine."

"That is a big family."

"We moved to Kilgore from New London after the big gas explosion at the school."

A vague memory of Texas history and oilfield disasters tugs at Ellis' consciousness.

"But that was a long time ago," she says. "And what about you?"

"Oh, I've lived in Kilgore my whole life."

"You're married," she says.

She says it as a certainty. But Ellis doesn't wear his wedding ring while on the job.

It's the quickest way to dislocate or even lose a finger messing with unstable pipes with sharp edges.

"I can just tell when a good man is married. There's a settled quality about him. It changes the contours of the face, the way he carries himself." She looks at him, her eyes alert and searching. He notices for the first time her necklace—long, ivory-colored pendants carved with indiscernible patterns and strung on a cord. Her knobby fingers stroke the worn surfaces in an intimate, and vaguely disturbing, way. The shape of the pendants is somehow familiar. . .

She laughs then. Not an old lady giggle, but the deep-throated laugh of a much younger woman. Her posture seems less bowed, the deep furrows across her forehead diminished. A trick of the softening light, Ellis thinks.

And the sunset is flaring to its final show of crimson and purple. It will be full on dark by the time he gets back to Kilgore after dropping his passenger off in Longview. He makes a mental note to call his wife soon, letting her know to hold up dinner for a half an hour or so.

"You can call your wife," she says, turning her head to look out the passenger side window. "Let her know you'll be late."

Ellis startles with the idea that she's been catching his thoughts. He stares at the back of her head. He can't see her face, but he gets the feeling that she's grinning at some hidden joke.

He takes out his phone and calls his wife, telling her he's carrying a lady he found stranded on the highway up to Longview. When he disconnects the call, Mathilda Belle Johnson is staring past him, taking in the last few moments of the sunset, her face bathed in its red light.

"You didn't touch them, did you?" she asks without looking at him.

"Touch what?"

"The things at Jerri Dean Conroe's place."

Now her eyes have found his, and a chill, as when he was stricken with scarlet fever as a boy, ripples through his body.

"No," he says. He remembers Donny decimating the worms with his bare feet, and Jerri Dean scooping them into the jelly jar with her fingers. He also remembers the boy scratching at the bottom of one foot, a look of concern etched into his face.

"Yes," she says softly, stretching out the last sibilant 's'. "It's dangerous to walk around this part of the country in your bare feet."

Ellis Hinton does not want to look at the old woman in that moment. He keeps his eyes pointed to the road. She's caught his thoughts again, and a sour tightening of his stomach that is nothing like indigestion cramps his middle. As a boy he did spend most of the year traipsing around the Piney Woods in his bare feet. And he'd had his share of encounters with scorpions, spiders, and red ants, as well as near misses with copperheads.

But he'd never in his life seen the likes of those thrusting, searching worms in the Conroe's back yard.

He increases the pressure on the gas pedal. The less time Mathilda Belle spends in his truck the better. The March evening air has begun to cool, but he's loath to close the windows. There's still that smell of something foul in the cab, and he's pretty sure at this point that it's not him.

How's the saying go, he wonders? No good deed goes unpunished.

"But how much more satisfying it is to punish the bad deed."

She must have moved in her seat because her voice sounds closer. Almost as though she's talking right into his ear. For the briefest moment, he wonders if he's been speaking his thoughts out loud. But he doesn't think so. All his limbs, his jaw and even his eyes seem nearly fixed and rigid. He can see the road ahead, and his right foot maintains pressure on the gas pedal, his hands gently correcting the wheel. But he might as well be a crash test dummy, controlled by the engineer sitting behind the observation window.

"'Vengeance is mine,' thus sayeth the Lord. At least that's what the faithful believers always say in the South, isn't it?" she asks.

"But us Southerners have also been known to say less charitable things when we've been greatly wronged like, 'I'll skin you alive', or 'I'll tear your arm off and beat you to death with it'."

Mathilda Belle chuckles, her breath hot in his ear. "Echoes and echoes of a darker, more ancient past. When women exacted their own vengeance."

She goes quiet for a moment, and Ellis begins to count the broken white lines on the shadowed highway to distract him from the certainty that she's going to elaborate on just what that vengeance looks like.

"You're too young to remember the New London School tragedy of 1937. But I was there when a gas explosion ripped apart almost three hundred students, some as young as eleven years old. I lost eight of my sisters on that day. I probably would have died too, except I was only ten and the first through fourth-graders had already been excused for the day."

She was ten years old in 1937, which meant she was ninety-two. He wanted to sneak another look at her but was unable to turn his head.

"Eighty-two years ago today, I sat in the playground waiting for my older sisters to be released, so we could all walk home together. It was a beautiful day on that 17th of March. We'd had lots of rainfall over the winter, so spring had already arrived in East Texas. At seventeen minutes past three in the afternoon, a sound like the end of the world broke across Rusk County, carrying for five miles in all directions. The walls of the school first bulged out like an overblown balloon. Then slabs of concrete, some the size of washing machines, were hurled into the air; one of them smashed on to a brand- new Chevy, crushing it flatter than a biscuit. The roof went off like a rocket. Roughnecks, many of them kin to the students, come from all over to help dig through the rubble with their bare hands. What they found under the tons of debris made even the most hardened of those oil field workers cry for their own mothers. Of my eight sisters lost, we had to identify all of them in pieces. Martha, my next oldest sister, had colored her toenails with a pink crayon the night before. We were too poor to buy nail polish, you see. My father identified her by her left foot. It was all that was left intact."

She pauses for a moment and wraps her fingers tightly around Ellis' arm.

"Can you imagine it?" she asks.

And he can imagine it. It's as though her touch is transmitting through his skin her own memories of the event. He sees the devastated building, the smashed cars, the roughnecks sweating and sobbing, their clothes covered in soot and ash and blood as they pull lumps of cement and steel away from small, pale bodies looking like so many broken dolls.

"I show you all this so you'll understand why we did what we did. My two sisters and I."

She removes her hand, and he's suddenly aware that his face is wet from tears. His breath is hitched and jagged as though he'd been crying for good long while.

"The explosion was caused by waste gas accumulating for who knows how long within the basement and walls of the building. The gas was odorless, so the teacher who started up the electric wood-shop sander didn't know that any spark was sure to ignite the conflagration.

"The whole winter before, the school had been heated with good, commercial grade gas. But come spring, the school trustees decided to save some money, so they had workers tap into a pipeline carrying waste gas produced by another, smaller refinery.

Imagine that. The best-endowed school in three counties, constructed at a cost of over a million dollars–which was a fortune in those days–was built from the wealth pumped out of the ground by oil barrens. And the school trustees, millionaires all, wanted to save a few hundred dollars a month.

"Jefferson, Miller, LeBeaux, Warner and Lawson. The names of the five trustees of the New London School. Any of those names sound familiar?"

The names did sound familiar to Ellis. The businesses, schools and cemeteries in Kilgore, and close neighboring towns like Overton and Gladewater, were filled people with those surnames. His best friend in high school, Bill Miller, had gotten into some trouble after graduation with drinking and drugs, and had died in a fiery car crash. One of his cousins had married a girl from the wealthy Lawson family. She'd taken a lethal overdose of pills after her affair with her fitness coach was made public.

If he really thought about it, he could probably lay claim to knowing lots of people who'd been born into those families. He'd gone to church with them. Had worked in their homes, attended their funerals, which, now that he thought about it some more, seemed disproportionate to other East Texas families.

Those five families were the First Families of East Texas and had all been made unimaginably rich from the oil and gas they sucked out of the red clay dirt. Their names were on buildings large and small. And they were stricken with the usual curses of the overly wealthy: addiction, infidelity, mendaciousness, and a seemingly tireless drive toward self-annihilation in general.

Ellis remembers when he was called to clear some pipes in the big LeBeaux mansion in Laird's Hill, a three-story, Victorian-style monstrosity, still owned and occupied by the aging daughter of the LeBeaux patriarch. After being greeted cordially by Priscilla LeBeaux, and given some lemonade and a moon pie, she excused herself, climbed up onto the roof and jumped off. Ellis held her hand, comforting her, until the ambulance arrived.

Her last words to him before she died were, "They made me do it, Ellis–"

They made me do it.

Finally, he's able to turn his head and he sees Mathilda Belle gazing peacefully into his eyes, but she hasn't moved closer to him at all. She strokes the pendants around her neck, and he counts ten of them.

I was one of eleven sisters, she had said.

"An inquest after the school explosion found that no one was to blame," she explains.

"It was simply an accident of nature. And Act of God, if you will. My sisters and I didn't see that as justice. No justice at all. Eighty-two years it's taken to even the scales.

My sisters and I working together for decades until Florence died, and then there were two. Then Anna died leaving one sister to finish our life's work. Mathilda Belle Johnson.

"We brought more with us from Charleston than suitcases, Mr. Hinton. We brought with us the Venus glass and haints and spells that were old when the pyramids were built."

Ellis stares at the ivory pendants again, the recognition of what they are refusing to coalesce inside his waking mind.

"Do you know what Jerri Dean Conroe's name was before she married?"

Ellis shakes his head.

"Jerri Dean Jefferson. She and her son were the last of the Jefferson line."

He's looking at the road again.

"Were," he croaks. "You said were the last."

In answer she exhales a long-satisfied sigh, as one will do after a particularly trying task is completed.

"But he's just a boy," Ellis says. In his mind's eye he sees Donny frenzied scratching at the place on his foot where the worms had touched.

"He's a twelve-year old with a killer's heart, and with a mother who pedals poison to children. The world will be a better place without them."

"What was that in the Conroe's sink?" he asks.

"Re-tri-bu-tion." She pulls out each syllable the way a preacher does when he shows his congregants the edges of the Fiery Pit.

His head feels like it's filled with helium, his chest tight, his left arm tingling as well.

Ellis Hinton thinks that he may be heading for an imminent heart attack. He thinks of all of his shortcomings, his defects of character, the many mean-spirited thoughts he had, over the years, directed at friends and family. Toward his own mother, especially after she had told him that his father was not his father. But, rather, that he was the son of a Warner family heir with whom his mother had had an affair.

"Who are you?" he asks, his voice breathy with fear.

She pats him on his thigh in a friendly way. "You're safe with me, Mr. Hinton.

You're a good man helping out a little old lady."

At her touch the tightness under his ribs dissipates, his vision sharpens again.

"We saved them where we could, my two sisters and I. The selfless, the kind, the compassionate, like yourself." She gives a short bark of laughter. "But they were in the woeful minority. . .Mr. Hinton turn left just here."

He realizes with a jolt that he has negotiated his way through the streets of Longview without being consciously aware that he had even entered the town limits.

She directs him to pull up to one of the modest houses facing the Grace Hill Cemetery, and, as though they'd been waiting for her to arrive, a group of young women and girls exit the house and stand on the porch in an expectant cluster.

"Mr. Hinton," she says, giving him a maternal smile. "Your profession has allowed you to see the worst of human excrescence. The hidden things that were never meant to see the light of day again, but which, like a bloated corpse, often rises to the surface again. I'm of a mind to see you as a sort of sentinel to the Underworld. One who illuminates to the living that the sins of the father can come back to infect the child.

That you have not been infected is a testament to your goodness. And why you'll go home to your wife tonight."

The women and girls approach only after Ellis has helped Mathilda Belle out of her seat. They gather around her, welcoming her, and then lead her carefully into the house.

The youngest of the group, a girl of about eight or so, stays behind to take charge of the shopping cart that Ellis has lifted from the back of the truck. She thanks him, smiles and wheels the cart into the house behind her sisters.

Ellis had counted eleven of them. He checks the name on the mailbox. The Baileys.

Eleven Bailey sisters, each one a mirrored image of the one who'd come before.

After calling in sick for a week, Ellis Hinton's first call back on the job is at the local middle school. A pipe in one of the science lab's sinks had backed up. Ellis completes the job quickly with the drain snake–some bright bulb had try to flush bits of paper down into the pipes–and he gathers up his tools, spending a few moments talking to the school's janitor who, as usual, gives him the gossip of the past few days: which kids have been arrested for mischief, which teachers are reportedly fooling around with which students, and so forth.

He also tells Ellis that after Donny Conroe's failure to show up for school for a few days, the sheriff stopped by their trailer and found both he and his mother dead from some as-yet-unknown disease. Evidently, according to the janitor, their bodies were swollen almost past recognition, and they had to be identified by their dental records.

The smell, he said, had been unbelievable.

As the janitor relates in lurid detail the state of the Conroe's remains, Ellis seeks to hide his growing horror at the news by turning away, pretending to check once more the counters and floor, as though he's making doubly sure he's not leaving anything behind.

His gaze rests on the replica of the anatomy skeleton in one corner, its skull rakishly adorned with a sombrero. He follows the attachments down, from the collarbone to the humerus, to the double bones of the forearm whose names he has forgotten, to the. . . phalanges. He's remembered the Latin name for the finger bones.

He now knows what the ninety-two-year-old Kilgore woman had been wearing around her neck. Ten cylindrical bones, a few yellowed with age, more blackened as though with a terrible heat, but all inscribed with mystic symbols. A bone taken from the hand of each one of the deceased and strung together as a necklace to adorn the last remaining sister–Mathilda Belle Johnson.

PESTILENCE

By Madison Estes

MY LEGS DANGLE OFF THE edge of the gynecologist's table. Sweat glues my bangs to my forehead. It must be a hundred degrees in here, and the pink tissue paper gown the nurse gave me starts to slide up my crack. Pamphlets with lovely, comforting headlines like "Living with HPV", "What You Need to Know about HIV" and "AIDS and How to Protect Yourself from STIs" greet me from across the room. I think of puppies, my biochem project, anything but those texts. As much as I try not to, I replay them again in my head.

I miss being inside you.
Been thinking about what I want to do to you all day.
You're still on the pill, right?
I wanna eat that ass. You into that?

The last one made me dry heave. I didn't even know people really did that outside of porn. I couldn't read anymore after that because Brian came back to my place once he realized he'd left his phone. He thought his secret was safe because he had a password-protected lock screen, but I snuck a peek at him entering the code when I started to get suspicious of all his late nights with the boys. I thought I was being paranoid, but weeks of sexting and dozens of naked pictures between him and a girl named Jasmine confirmed my suspicions. The next day, I scheduled an appointment to get checked out.

When the doctor comes in, she smiles and seems to be just the right amount of cheerful and professional for someone who is about to look up my coochie. This friendly, middle-aged woman introduces herself and starts asking me about my sexual history.

"How many partners have you had in the past year?"

I want to tell her, "Look, I've only been with one person, but it might as well have been a dozen, because every person he had sex with increased my chance of getting an STD. I didn't consent to all these risks. I just believed my boyfriend when he said he only wanted to be with me, and that we didn't have to keep it safe because we were being exclusive."

Instead I mumble, "Just one."

"Did you use protection?"

"No. I'm on the pill." Her lips turn downward. Medical professionals aren't supposed to be judgmental, but there's a concern-bordering-disappointment look in her eyes that reminds me of my mother.

"We were supposed to be monogamous," I say.

She frowns harder. "Monogamy is for penguins."

I want to tell her that research has shown that some female penguins may have one to three partners in one season and some males may have one or two partners, but I hold my tongue.

She doesn't want to hear Animal Planet facts, and I don't want to be here any longer than necessary. I put my legs in the cold metal stirrups and scoot down towards the edge of the table. I try to ignore the paper gown crawling further up my ass. She swabs my vagina. My eyes shoot to the tile ceiling. Thin black marks spot the white ceiling, hundreds of them spiraling, like bacteria swimming under a microscope. I don't want to see these spots that look like the germs that are probably inside of me. I wish they had put a T.V. on the ceiling so I could watch something mindless like The Big Bang Theory and pretend this wasn't happening to me.

The pelvic exam is worse. She doesn't heat up the speculum before she inserts it and she uses the wrong size and it hurts more than losing my virginity to a guy I was smart enough to wear a condom with and I want to scream, but I bite my fist instead. She's punishing me. She's punishing me, and maybe I deserve it for being so stupid.

I can't wait to be inside you again. You're the best I've ever had. Tomorrow night?

I haven't prayed in several years, but I say a prayer now. God, please let everything be okay. Don't let me be infected. I'll do anything.

"We're almost done here," the gynecologist says, noting my discomfort. When I look down, I nearly scream again, because it's not the nice woman I met moments ago, but a hooded figure in a white robe between my legs, peering down at my opening. Something icy penetrates me, even colder than the stirrups. My chest feels too tight to yell, so I whisper, "No. Stop. Please."

Why didn't I say that sooner? Why didn't I say that to Brian before I let him have sex with me without a condom?

I squeeze my eyes shut from the pain, and when I open them, the robed figure is gone.

The gynecologist disposes of her latex gloves and gives me a sympathetic smile.

"We should get the results back in two weeks," she says. "Try not to worry in the meantime."

As I drive home, I pass almost a dozen churches. It's impossible not to when you live in South Texas. I stop at a pitiful, run-down church because it is the only one with a door open in the middle of the week. When I get to the front, I see that the door isn't open but missing. The church is deserted, the congregation likely dispersed among other various religious organizations in the community. It's for the best. I don't need confession or support right now; I need God.

I go to the altar and pray for God to have mercy on my body and soul.

As I toss and turn in my bed, trying to sleep, the shrouded figure returns. He brings others with him, all in different colored cloaks: white, red, black, and pale green. I open my mouth to scream, but nothing comes out. My chest constricts. I can't move. The black veiled figure removes its hood, revealing an oblong skull, triangular and definitely not human. It turns its head to the side, examining me. A dozen square teeth peek out in a lopsided grin. I don't recognize what it is at first because it's so thin that it reminds me of dinosaur skeletons I once saw on a museum field trip. It's only when one of its hairy hoofs emerges from the cloak and touches one of the others that I realize what they are.

The four horsemen.

I didn't think they would literally be part-horse, like a reverse centaur. They don't speak to me or each other. They communicate in hoof gestures and neighing. They seem to get on the same page and spread out across the room.

I'm not in my bedroom anymore. I'm in a hospital. There are three other beds lined up in a row with a girl on each. One of them looks half-starved. Her ribs protrude. Her waist is a sheet of paper. Her cheeks are sunken in like a mummy. One horseman puts its black hooves between her thighs and spreads her skinny legs. She doesn't resist. Her eyes roll back into her head like she's going to pass out as he enters her. Somehow I know, perhaps from all the Sunday school lessons that were drilled into my head as a child, that this is famine.

She is famine.

The next girl is a petite blonde who fights the cloaked figure taking her on the bed. Her eyebrows furrow in distress as it stomps her chest, leaving hoof prints all over her breasts. It discards its red robe onto the floor. Red is supposed to mean something, but I can't remember what. Blood, maybe. Or carnage. Violence. I see blood between her legs, scratches all along her arms and torso from where its hooves are pushing her down into the mattress. She scratches back. They are fighting; they are at war.

She is war.

The last girl doesn't move. Doesn't open her eyes. The horseman drops its pale green cloak to reveal human-like legs, but its genitals look more horse than man. The long pink organ protrudes from its brown sheath. I feel sick. Bile rises in my throat. What is she? I go back to my Sunday school days, coloring in pictures of Noah's ark, answering trivia questions about

Adam and Eve, receiving that abstinence ring that I should have taken more seriously, but nothing pertinent comes back to me about the four horsemen until I see the maggots squirming on her body. The thrusting motion as he enters her over and over seems to have awakened them, energized them.

Death. She is death.

Finally, the horseman before me removes its white cloak. It neighs, and this naked half- man, half-horse braying would be comical if its erect horse cock didn't look like it would split me in half. I look away and see that the horseman plunging into Famine seems to match her in thinness. It shrinks the more it pounds into her. Both the horseman of war and its victim are glazed in each other's blood as they fight and fuck. The horseman of death is covered in maggots and flies now; insects of decomposition pour out of them, and they stink of rot. Bile rises again. I turn and puke over the side of the bed. It doesn't deter my horseman in the least. Which one is this? I can't remember. Famine. War. Death. Why can't I remember the last one?

It comes to me when the horseman sticks his jutting cock near my face. It does its best to guide it into my vomit-coated mouth with its hooves. Even more appalling than the animalistic genitals are the warts and blisters that cover it. I jerk my head away. Inflamed blisters rub against my lips. One of them bursts from the friction. The pus oozes against my mouth and drips down my chin. If I scream, he'll shove the whole thing in, so I whimper instead. I try to be strong and resist, but the stench coming from Death makes me gag. The horseman takes this opportunity to shove the disease-ridden cock inside my mouth. The blisters rip open on my teeth, spilling into my mouth. As I choke, I remember it at last.

Pestilence. I am pestilence.

I wake up drenched in sweat. The horsemen and their victims visit me every night as I wait for the test results. Waiting is the hardest part, especially when you already know what the outcome will be. I try to imagine a phone call with good news, but instead, I remember more texts.

Show me that ass again. I want to see what I'm gonna be wrecking tonight.

You should be a model. For real, you're so hot. I wish every girl had a body like you. My last girl was a skinny twig, no ass at all.

I'm going to fuck you so good tonight, baby.

I am the skinny twig, no ass girl he was talking about, only I wasn't his last girl when he sent that text. I was, or still am, his current girl. I haven't told him I know yet. I'm still figuring out how to go about it.

I think about confronting him at the Good Ol' Boy's Country Bar he works at. It's a family-owned bar. He'd be humiliated. But if I confronted him publicly, he'd say I was crazy and it would make him look like a victim. Everyone would feel sorry for him. He'd use me as a sob story to get into the next girl's pants.

I think about stealing his phone and sending all the sexts and nudes to his family and friends. Would any of them even care? Do I even care if they care at this point?

I think about handcuffing him to the headboard and pouring acid on his sad little limp dick, watching it curl and shrivel as the chemical eats away at his flesh like salt corroding a snail.

I think about this most of all. Pestilence appears beside me, nodding in approval as I allow the dark fantasy to play in my head. All it would take to lure him here are pictures of me in black lingerie and a text saying, "Hey baby, what are you doing tonight?"

Pestilence nods again. Open sores and weeping abscesses cover its face. I feel an itch between my legs. I put the phone down and hop in the shower, trying to wash this gross feeling away. To get some relief, I use a douche and scrub a soapy loofah between my legs. When I open the shower curtain, my visitor is gone.

I wake up clawing at my vaginal lips with my nails. I itch so badly that I scratched myself raw in my sleep. Once I'm in the shower, I try to wash away the pus and contamination.

I want to skin myself and sterilize the insides. I would have scrubbed my flesh with bleach if it wouldn't have left burns. Regular soap can't get me clean. Not in a way that I can feel it. I switch to hypoallergenic soap because I am washing myself several times a day, and I don't want to dry my skin out and create new problems. But lavender and vanilla-scented baby soap can't take away the feeling of disease, or the stench of Brian, perspiring and filthy as he moved above me, inside me, and filthy, the repugnant odor of his testicles hovered all around me so filthy. He never showered enough, preferring to cover his stench with cheap cologne. He was scum from the start. The word repeats in my head, like the chanting you hear in Catholic church ceremonies, the ones where they anoint you with oil. Only instead of oil, mud is smeared along my face, all over my body, and all I see is

filth filth filth

Brian has been ignoring my calls and texts. I drive to The Good Ol' Boy's Country Bar and wait in the parking lot. He walks out with Jasmine, and they are all over each other. She rubs her faux leather cowgirl boots against his calf and wraps her arms around him. For a moment, I think I might just go. They deserve each other, and I already feel like a crazy stalker showing up at his job unannounced. As they get closer, the light from the neon sign illuminates their faces.

He's not with Jasmine. He's with a girl I've never even seen before, and he's about to get to second base with her right here in the parking lot.

Pestilence sits in the passenger's seat. A large medical mask covers its face. I can't tell if that's to protect me from it or it from me. Its boils and blisters have multiplied since the last time I saw it, but so have mine. The red bumps between my vaginal lips that were calming down start to flare up. The itching and burning intensifies. I weep, scratching my crotch as he makes out with this girl against his car.

When I get home, I put on my sexiest bra and panty set and take selfies from the neck down, still crying. The lacy material aggravates my already delicate skin, and I can't get the image of him and this new girl out of my head. I send him the pictures and a text. Miss me?

He sends back a gentleman's only proper response: an unfiltered dick pic, and for some reason, an unnatural emphasis on his scrotum.

See you 2nite.

When he gets to my house, two hours later, he flashes what he believes must be an irresistible grin. I want to retch as I think about him with the girl in the pink boots. His features seem warped now, his smile crooked and full of secrets, his eyes beady instead of warm. How did I ever find him attractive?

"I would like you to pray with me," I tell him. He laughs.

"Very funny." He slides his hands around my back, pressing himself against me. I gag when I smell cheap perfume and push him away.

"We need to get our souls right with God. That's the only way to avoid his punishment."

"What's going on?" he asks. "You sent me those pics, basically asked me to come fuck you, now you're pushing me away? Are you trying to play hard to get?"

Pestilence snorts, smashes a hoof against the wall, but Brian can't see or hear my other guest.

"If we both repent, maybe we can become clean again."

Another laugh. "This is a roleplay thing, isn't it? You're a good Catholic school girl? I'm a bad boy, coming to corrupt you?"

"Something like that."

I look at the mounted horseshoe he gave me when we first started dating. I didn't know he'd stolen it from his family's country-themed bar when he gave it to me. At the time, I thought it was cute in a rustic way. It reminded me of when we first started dating, of twilight picnics and blanket fort movie nights. Before the lies and excuses and humiliation of having my vagina swabbed because of him. I pull the horseshoe off and turn it upside down, spilling out all the good luck it never brought me.

"What are you doing with that old thing?" he asks. The horseshoe is rusted and tarnished—I'll probably need a tetanus shot considering how hard I grab it when I bash it into the back of Brian's skull. I sigh in relief when I feel his pulse beneath my fingers. I'm not sure what I have planned will work if he dies first.

Maybe the horseshoe is good luck after all.

I rub olive oil and recite prayers over Brian's unconscious body. He comes to with a groan. His eyebrows furrow. He is confused about why he's chained to a post in my shed, with translucent plastic covering the space from floor to ceiling.

"What's going on? How did I get here?" he says.

"I had some help."

Pestilence sits beside me in a yellow hazmat suit, its face obstructed by a gas mask. I'm wearing thick gloves and plastic over my clothes, not to hide evidence but because I don't want any more contact with Brian. My hands were coated in invisible grime the moment they made contact with his bare skin. I washed them several times before donning some gloves and protective clothing to shield me from him. I only wish I'd always handled him with his much caution, but back then, I didn't know his penis was a Petri dish of bacteria and disease.

"Allison? Alli? What's going on? Is this some weird new sex game you wanna play?"

"You wish."

Pestilence tilts its head back and brays, impatient. I dab my glove into the oil and smear it against Brian's forehead.

"What are you doing?"

"Anointing you."

I unzip his jeans and pull them off. I pull out his penis and rub the oil over it. Despite his terror and, to my annoyance, he gets half-hard before I'm done.

"I'm so confused," he says.

"Don't worry. It'll be over soon." I turn on my laptop and place it within his view. A loud laugh track fills the room.

"Why are you doing this to me?" He yanks against his restraints.

"Hey, at least you get to watch The Big Bang Theory. That's more than I got."

"Please. I love you, baby. Whatever this is, we can work through it."

Against my will, the good times flash before my eyes, first kisses and holidays and surprise vacations. I frown, looking over at Pestilence for support. It tilts its head as if to say, "So what?" I hesitate.

"Okay," I say at last, reaching up toward the ropes that bind him.

"Really?" His eyes close in relief.

I lean in close to him and whisper in his ear.

"Bazinga."

Before he has time to process what I said, I pull out the scalpel.

"What? What are you going to—Oh God, don't do that—"

The blade meets the base of his penis. With a flick of my wrist, the root is almost severed from his pelvis. It hangs on by a thin strand of skin and muscle. I rectify this with a second swipe, and remove the infected genitals. It isn't covered in warts and blisters like Pestilence and me, but there is no doubt in my mind that this three-inch (and I'm being generous here) innocent- looking flaccid piece of skin and tissue is contaminated, the culprit behind my rashes and itching.

I offer the afflicted organ to Pestilence, giving it the honor of destroying the cursed thing. The horseman removes the gas mask, opens its mouth, and takes it. Pestilence chomps down on it before swallowing. Bits of flesh hang between its long, yellow teeth when it smiles.

"Not how I thought you were going to get rid of it, but okay," I say.

It gives a half-whine, half-laugh. A dark red pool forms around Brian, and he passes out from the pain and blood loss. The Big Bang Theory laugh track plays again after Leonard makes another crack about Sheldon's antics. I chuckle along with it.

An hour later, I'm still itching. The ritual didn't work. I thought ridding the world of a proud, unapologetic disease spreader might grant my own body some mercy from this affliction, but God is angrier than I thought, or I misunderstood what I was supposed to do. Perhaps Pestilence tricked me. But I don't have time to focus on that. I have a body to get rid of.

Dismemberment takes longer than I thought it would. Castration is easy compared to cutting through bones, even with an old hacksaw I picked up from a pawnshop. The acid composition from my biochem class does the rest, although it dissolves much slower than Google said it would.

I take his hands and gently set them inside the acid, careful that it doesn't splash, although I have goggles and a face mask on just in case it does. My phone vibrates.

"Hello, is this Allison?"

I confirm my birthday and first and last name.

"I just wanted to tell you that your results all came back negative. We recommend annual pap smears for women your age, so if you want, we can schedule your next appointment right now—"

"Excuse me, you said the results were negative?"

"That's right."

"All of them?" My mouth hangs open.

Brian's bloody arm drips on my white shoes. His hands sizzle in the acid. An index finger seems to point at me, right before it collapses in the mush.

"Yes. It came back negative for HIV, Herpes, HPV . . ." she lists off every sexually transmitted disease known to man. "All negative".

"But I've been itching down there like crazy. It's all red and bumpy."

"Have you used any new soaps or detergents?"

"I don't think so. Just hypoallergenic soap, but that's like . . . hypoallergenic."

"What about new lubricants or douches?"

I groan.

"I'm a douche."

"Excuse me?"

"I said it was probably the douche."

I try to listen to what she says next, but it's so hard to pay attention with Brian's tongue sticking out like those dogs that have all their teeth removed.

"Yes, we get a lot of girls that have issues due to douches," the woman from the clinic continues. "It disrupts the pH balance and can cause yeast infections. We recommend using an over-the-counter cream, and if you'd like to come in again for another exam, we can schedule you for next week."

"I'm going to have to call you back." I stare at the top and bottom halves of my ex- boyfriend. "I'm sort of in the middle of something."

THE LAST TABOO

By Jess Hagemann

HER BREATH SMELLED LIKE COMMUNION wafers. Something yeasty and cold I could crawl inside, feast upon, and feel content. Hovering inches from mine, her lips like fat pink grubs. Her breasts two cheesecloth sacks of yogurt I might spend a lifetime savoring. As June shimmied and shook, the tassels on her auburn nipples swinging, I tried to remember if she'd always been this beautiful. In high school, had the boys eaten out of her hand? And before that—was she a daddy's girl, my sister? Had that grown man stared at her like the men in this room? Whistling and drooling in the dark, our little audience, come to witness the last taboo?

The other, our third, was spinning suspended on the pole. One strong thigh slipped around its greased length, laughing at gravity. Her right leg stuck straight out, a ballerina's, point-toed. Mesmerized, I went to her, hips swaying along with the music. Dropping to my knees, I pulled her blue sequined thong aside with my teeth. I worshipped there, accepting her communion. A sacrament as old as time. For a while, after the procedure, she'd tasted differently. But now she was Sue again. The Sue I'd loved since childhood.

It was Dan's idea. "The Striplets," he'd said, running a hand through the air like he was spelling out the name in lights. "Triplets, who strip—and more." Crossing his arms and grinning, already raking in the money in his head. Then all of it jeopardized last spring, when Sue had missed her period, the men who pay us to fuck each other not the same men who pay to ogle pregnant bodies. And now me in the same boat. Needing the same Boat.

Yes, I nodded, when Sue asked me with her eyes. So after the show was over and the back room cleared out, after Dan had counted out our cash and raided his own bar, we got in Sue's car. She drove me south along the same highway she'd driven herself last May. June hadn't gone then, and she didn't come with us now. She didn't want to know, she said. She needed to recharge.

We were quiet the whole way, the stars above talking enough for both of us. Cygnus spread her swan wings, an invitation, and Sagittarius flirted back from his horse. They played out the drama we'd been trained to play, the imperative we'd pursued. I thought Sue might ask me *who* or *when* or *why* or *how*, but all she asked, three hours later, was, "Ready?" The Gulf had come into view. Its salt-waves, black beneath the moon, tongued the shore. In the distance, our destination. The yacht with winking eyes, with all the answers.

The number had changed since she'd come here alone, but Sue knew how to find what we needed. She texted the password, waited, read the response. Was she the smart daughter, I wondered, when we were little? The one who never messed up, until someone messed her up? I couldn't remember.

"They're coming," she said at the moment I saw the boat, not the yacht but the speedboat that would ferry me to it. I said I wanted her to come. I couldn't do it by myself, not like her, the smart *and* the strong one. She said she wasn't sure if they'd let her. She might be perceived as a threat. "But we're *sisters*," I pointed out. "Anyone can see that." It didn't occur to me that that was the problem. Or that, in coming aboard, Sue would have to remember—be forced, unlike June, to know.

The man who took us in the speedboat had no face. At least, I'd be unable to recall it, later, after my taste had changed, then changed back. They looked the same, though, I think, almost like triplets. The one who drove the boat, and the two who held me down inside.

"How far along are you?" one wearing a medical mask and gloves asked.

"Eight weeks?" I guessed and shrugged.

"And who's the father?"

"His name is Dan."

The mask typed the name into his system. Pulled up a chart, read. Sue squeezed my hand.

"When was your last update?"

I consulted my own files. "Yesterday."

The mask blinked, satisfied.

A new man entered the makeshift exam room, four blank walls, table, reclining chair. He held a wand slathered in jelly. It whistled and drooled through the air. "Deep breath," he coached me, as the cold wand crawled inside. He left its greased length there, to savor my yogurt, to confirm how I had been desecrated. A sacrament as old as time.

Collectively, we waited for a heartbeat we'd never hear.

Sue's legs, I noticed, stuck straight out, point-toed. Her arms on the table beside me rigid and unbending. I tried to conjure an early image. Had she been born that way, her limbs taking up all the room in our womb? The mask had plugged a cord into her toe, was busy toggling something on, erasing something else. Immobilized, she was nevertheless awake and aware. Sue knew, and now I did, too. I watched the new man turn a vacuum on, bring its plastic tubing my way.

Will it hurt? I should have asked Sue, but it was too late. Her frame lay slack again. They'd rewritten her, and soon they would rewrite me. Of the three of us, only June would retain her original code. Her innocence. Only June would remain intact. Sue and I, we were automatons, purpose-built and rebuilt each time Dan failed to control himself. He never touched June. She was too beautiful, intimidatingly so, the best of a body produced in triplicate. The consummate daddy's girl.

My wires disconnected from my waist down, I couldn't feel, could only see, the tissue they sucked from my internal cavity. It was yellow and globular—or that's how it appeared as it slurped up the plastic tubing. Perhaps, I reasoned, I'd always been the funhouse striplet. The maze people chased their desire into, the hall of mirrors reflecting their wildest fantasies. In my rotating barrel, you could lose your lunch or find a nonviable fetus, a metastasizing flesh lump. Me, a hollow projection. Anything you wanted me to be.

Next to me, Sue rebooted. She stood up and walked to the porthole window, the only one in the room. "I can see The Three Sisters," she said, which made me smile—even though in some cultures, they're known as Orion's Belt: an accessory for another man, like Dan. I smiled because they laughed at gravity. Because, ballerinas all, stars never stopped dancing. We talked about what June was probably doing. Washing her tassels in the sink, maybe. Watching makeup tutorials.

After the vacuum, there was scraping. A metal spoon with serrated edges "to make sure we got it all." I heard the wet emptying, like guts pulled from a pumpkin at Halloween. Like a grooming cat, content.

When I was done, the faceless man ferried us back to the dock. "No work for a week," he cautioned. "And next time, be more careful." As if I controlled what happened to me. As if any of us had a choice.

Back on the road, Sue asked how I was doing. Did I need anything? She could stop at a gas station.

"Turn left," I said, because left was west. Was away from Dan and June and home.

But Sue scoffed, mistaking my plea for a joke. Her guffaw tinkled, was the only answer.

And so, we played out the drama we'd been trained to play, that our programming required.

LONELY DEATH ON A WEDNESDAY, 1 PM, AT A MOTEL OUTSIDE MARFA

By Emma E. Murray

LYLA SAT UNDER THE UMBRELLA and stared at the blue waves lapping the slimy walls of the pool. Leaning back, she took small sips of her orange juice, pretending it was a mimosa, or some other drink she'd seen grown women order at bars. She stretched out her arms, checking that her tan had not crossed over into sunburn, before turning her eyes back to the pool.

Beneath the surface of the water, the young boy's arms flailed. His head was bent back; dark bangs half-covered his wild, glassy eyes while he fought, gasping, to stay above the water.

She thought he was surprisingly quiet, considering the situation.

She'd watched his mom slather him in sunscreen, then disappear through the gate, back into the cool dark of one of the nearby motel rooms. As the water swirled around him, the oil slick of sunscreen on the surface caught the light and danced atop each undulation. His small mouth would reappear every few seconds, gaping like a fish, barely making a sound before it sank back below the surface. His legs pedaled beneath him, as if he were riding an invisible bicycle.

The boy reminded her of a frog.

As his head slipped under for the final time, Lyla leaned forward, straining to see his face and what expression he might wear during these last moments, but bubbles obscured her view.

Then, he stopped moving altogether.

Pulling down her sunglasses and crawling on her knees to the end of the lounge chair, she could better see his body bobbing vertically just below the surface. She scanned his face. There was no expression at all. Blank and pallid, his hair still covering his eyes, he was no longer a person. Just a body.

She finished her juice and dropped the empty plastic bottle on the ground. With her eyes on the boy, she walked the perimeter of the pool, passed through the gate, and up the concrete steps to the comfort of her own dark, air-conditioned room.

Her mom was exactly as she'd left her, on her back and snoring, splayed across the unmade bed. The rim of yellow-green under one eye— a thin, almost healed crescent—made her shudder. Lyla was supposed to wake her after only twenty minutes, but now it'd been well over an hour. Standing at the side of the bed, Lyla poked her mother's side with a finger.

"You gotta wake up now. We need to leave," Lyla whispered, pushing her mom's hair behind her ear, but she only stirred in her sleep. Lyla repeated it, pressing her mouth against her mother's ear, who woke with a start.

"Was I snoring again? I'm sorry," her mother said, yawning and turning to the bedside table and checking the clock. "Oops, overslept. I thought you were going to wake me up?" She smiled and stretched before her sleepy eyes registered the hint of distress painted across Lyla's brow. "What's wrong?"

"I told you, we've gotta leave," the girl said. "The police'll probably come soon. A boy drowned in the pool."

"What? What did you say?" Her mother's lip quivered; eyes wide.

"A boy drowned in the pool. Out front. I saw. Nobody else was there, but I'm sure somebody will notice soon. Then the cops will come."

"Oh my god, you watched this? Are you alright?"

She sat up straight and grabbed her daughter's hands, clutching them together between her own, but Lyla merely shrugged, her expression unchanged.

"I guess we should start packing. We need to leave. Probably best to get into New Mexico, or even old Mexico, quick as we can, don't ya' think?" Lyla asked, her voice calm as she pulled her hands through her blonde hair. Her mother nodded, confused and still half-asleep.

Lyla walked around the still-dark room, picking up various pieces of clothing and shoving them into suitcases. Her mom joined in the silent cleanup, stopping to fold each piece before slipping it into the bag and drying the toiletries before packing them away. She even picked up the dirty towels from the puddle on the floor.

Within five minutes, they were ready to leave. Her mom checked under the skirt of the bed, to make sure nothing had been kicked under, while Lyla heaved both bags over her shoulders and carried them down the stairs to the car.

She popped the trunk and tossed them inside before turning toward the pool, which waited across the empty parking lot. No one seemed to have noticed the boy was missing yet, and this thought stung like a cramp in her chest. Lyla exhaled slowly, focusing on her breathing and the feeling began to fade.

She couldn't see the boy from where she stood. She wanted to see him again, to assure herself of his reality, but before she could, the door banged shut above her. The sound of her mother's sandals across the concrete breezeway cut through the quiet, hot air. If she looked over the upstairs railing, would she see the small body floating alone?

Lyla didn't want her mother to look. This had been only hers to witness; a secret thing, and she felt an absurd urge to protect the boy's privacy from her nosy mom. The soft slapping of her mother's flip-flops paused briefly, then the slapping began again, starting down the stairs.

Anger bubbled within the girl.

She knew her mother had seen him. Lyla slammed the trunk closed and took her place in the passenger seat, reclining the chair as far as possible, her legs crossed and bare feet resting on the dash. Her mom opened the driver's door and dropped a couple odds and ends she'd found in the empty cupholder.

"Wait here. Gotta turn in the key card."

Her mother marched quickly across the parking lot to the small office that had been so cold with both the fan and the air conditioner blasting, the melodramatic voices of a telenovela blaring on the TV perched in the corner. Through the windshield, she could see the sleepy-eyed receptionist wave at her mother, and Lyla wished she could stay with him instead. Anyone but mom, anywhere but this car.

It took only a moment, and then they were pulling out onto US 90 again. Lyla couldn't help but look back to the pool, still and lifeless, its concrete baking in the high afternoon sun as they headed further into the desert.

They drove without speaking for a long time. Her mother turned on the radio, but when Lyla drew her knees up and faced the window, she quickly turned it off again.

"I wonder how long until somebody finds him," Lyla said, trying to sound casual, but her voice was thick with phlegm.

"I mean, it can't be too long before his mother realizes and starts looking for him, right?" her mom asked, looking back and forth between her daughter's face and the road.

"I don't know. It's already been a while as it is. Maybe she wished this would happen. Maybe that's why she left him alone."

But that wasn't true, Lyla realized. The boy's mother hadn't exactly left him alone; she'd left him with her. Her stomach dropped and her skin turned clammy and cold, dotted with goosebumps.

Not one word had been uttered; not one glance exchanged between her and the boy's mother. For all she knew, his mother hadn't even noticed her there and assumed the pool was empty. The umbrellas and chairs had certainly obscured her from view as she'd observed them.

She'd watched his mother dutifully slather stripes of white across his small tan body, and he'd jumped in right away, completing thwarting her attempts at sun protection. The mother had shouted something, threw down the sunscreen, and then was gone. No cheers for the boy's excellent cannonball, no laughter at his rambunctious hijinks, nothing that a loving parent would do. Just the seething resentment every mother has for children doomed to disappoint.

Had she seen her? No, she couldn't have noticed Lyla at the edge of the pool, quietly drinking her orange juice. Even if she'd seen her, she could never identify her. Nor would she need to, for it was the mother's negligence, not her own, that had resulted in the boy's death.

Still, Lyla's heart pounded against her ribcage in a rapid, painful rhythm.

"Well, that's a sad thought, if that's true," her mom said, eyes focused on the road. The girl stretched out her legs; her expertly painted blue toenails sparkled in the sun, touching the glass.

"Come on, don't smudge up the windshield."

Lyla acted as if she hadn't heard her.

Thick silence surrounded them like a fog as the miles rolled by. Finally, her mother's sharp, tinny voice carved through it. "Are you okay? That must've been a hard thing to see."

She shrugged, but her mind was busy weighing every conversation the two had ever had, every give and take of trust between them.

"I feel a little bad I didn't help him."

Her mom nodded then sucked in her lips, thinking before she answered. "Well, why didn't you help him?"

"It's not like I could've done anything. I'm not a lifeguard. He could've pulled me under!

Then we both would've died." The wave of excuses crashed out of Lyla with more emotion than she'd expected. She scowled at her mom, her face flushing a deep red.

Her mom's gaze stayed forward, forever on the road, but Lyla knew she was watching.

Seconds passed as slowly as hours. Silence built its heavy wall around them again.

"You're right, you're not a lifeguard, but you could've gotten help. You know, he might've even lived if you'd acted quick enough." She watched her mom tiptoe across the words, eyes still avoiding her, glued to the road.

"I suppose I could've. But his mom shouldn't have left him alone like that."

"Something must have happened. I'm sure she was coming right back."

"Yeah, just like we told Dad. We'd be right back."

Lyla took pleasure in watching her mom wince.

Her mother's hands gripped the wheel until they were bone white. Lyla knew she wanted to slam on the brakes, scream and slap her face over and over to remind her of what she'd saved her from, but she didn't dare. Lyla held all the power in her back pocket where the phone remained switched off and silent, patiently waiting to be brought back to life.

Instead, she bit her tongue and kept her eyes ahead of her, telling herself: only a little longer and then they could stop hiding. Things could finally get better. Just a little longer, and the girl would realize she was wrong, finally embrace the truth. The fragile mending of their relationship could begin.

Lyla looked back at her toenails, lagoon blue with sparkly flecks flashing in the sun, painted just days ago by her grandmother. Her father's mother, who she may never see again.

The thought shot a bolt of pain through her gut.

Her pocket held eternities of conversations with her friends, pictures taken with her cousins, calendar reminders of soccer practice with Dad every Thursday, always followed by their tradition of milkshakes at Whataburger, and all the other things she loved that would never happen again if she chose to protect her mom. If she didn't make that call. Then she thought of the boy in the pool again, but this time her heart lurched, urging her to somehow turn back time.

She almost let herself cry, but the dry air swept away any tears that attempted to form. Instead, her face felt unbearably hot. She rolled down the window, taking deep breaths of the sunbaked land, a sickening whiff of a dead skunk they'd passed wafting just below the surface.

Stifling the howling wail rising inside her throat, she thought of the boy and his stupid, useless mother, who had been worried about all the wrong things. That mother, alone with her son, at a motel in the middle of nowhere, forcing him to swim and play by himself. She pictured him bobbing in the pool, his face blank beneath the surface, and though her body ached with regret, she envied how he no longer had to choose. He would never have to choose again.

He could be free.

GARDEN DIRT AND HILL COUNTRY WINE

By Jae Mazer

MY MOM HAS A DIFFICULT time cooking a meal. Maybe she's distracted, absentminded, or sometimes outright disgusted with the food, or the process, or god knows what. But for whatever reason—as she chops, measures, stirs, plates—there's always a pause. And sometimes that pause lingers into an all-out stall that swells into full abandonment.

"Mom?"

Mom stops what she's doing, which isn't chopping the carrots on the cutting board but rather staring at them with her brow scrunched, eyes slits. The sound of my voice does not reignite the chopping, but her gaze moves from the carrots on the cutting board to the window above.

The chicken in the oven is well on its way to being cooked, and the potato water belching steam threatens to soften the root-veg within to absolute mush. Those carrots need to be cut and cooked soon if we want to serve them with dinner.

Mom's dinners were legendary—good ole fashioned cook-up with chicken-fried steak, fresh veggies from the garden, topped off with a decadent pecan pie made with the pecans from our very own hickory tree growing at the back of our land. I miss those meals. I miss Mom.

"Earth to Mom," I say, and I set my wineglass down on the island a little too hard.

Outside, a dog barks. Then howls. It matches the bray from the nursery upstairs. My son didn't sleep for long this time. Seems he sleeps less and less these days.

"Remi needs in," Mom says, but she is no longer looking out the window. And she's not looking at the carrots. She is staring at her hands, at the striations there, road maps of her age and experiences.

"Okay," I say. Frustrated. "Do you want me to let him in?"

"Yes."

Her hands are still. The carrots remain half cut.

"Are you busy?" I ask, hoping to spur her into action.

She doesn't answer. Or move.

I get up and go to the back door. Remi, Mom's 12-year-old German Shepherd, is standing in the middle of the yard, hackles raised, staring. Just like Mom is staring at her hands.

"Remi, come!" I call.

Remi hesitates. His back end quavers as bad as his voice. Remi is an old boy, and his hips aren't so good anymore. I think he's holding on because he knows Mom needs him, especially since Dad passed two summers ago. Eventually, Remi trots over and comes inside, then disappears somewhere deeper in the house. Next to Granny Bea in the parlor, I figure. The sound of his nails ticking across the hardwood and Gran's knitting needles colliding are a complementary percussion in the near distance. I go to Mom and the carrots. Place my hand on hers.

"Mom."

She pulls her hand away.

"I'm okay," she says. "Just tired."

It's not just tired. I worry about dementia, about misfiring synapses, even psychosis. There is fear on her face that I can't explain and that she won't.

"How can I help you if you won't talk to me?" I say.

Mom snaps at me. As she does.

"There is nothing wrong with me!"

"I didn't say there was." Even though there is.

"I'm tired," she repeats.

Me too. That's motherhood, though, right? Permanent exhaustion, compassion fatigue, a dwindling well of saintly patience. But I'm grown and an only child, and Mom has no one left to care for, save the infant grandchild who is still too little to be away from my breast for long.

Texas families are big, but ours is so very small. I wonder if Mom longs for more. Like I do.

The click-clack-clicking of Granny Bea's knitting needles in the other room provides a tempo for the crescendoing wail upstairs. My son's cry rings in my ears, a wordless screech that somehow shrieks the word Mom in its own language. Repeating it, over and over again, demanding a response. The front of my shirt soaks as my nipples respond to the sound before I do.

"Fuck." The word sticks in my throat like a lump of cornbread.

I cannot cry anymore. I refuse. My little boy upstairs does enough crying for all of us.

"Cut the carrots."

Mom's voice, so direct and so clear, startles me. She doesn't often make eye contact, but she is now, and the thick grey of her irises transfixes me.

"What?" I say. "I have to … He's hungry."

"He won't die," Mom says. "It'll do him good to learn to wait. I will go and read him a story."

Mom doesn't wait for me to agree to this plan. She turns on her blocky heels and clops out of the kitchen, down the hall, and up the stairs—clip, clop, clip—as she moves to the nursery above me. The wailing bounces, jiggles, and softens.

She's holding him. He is safe. He won't die if I take just a moment.

I pick up the knife and start chopping. The sound is so loud, and every time the blade slices through a carrot and makes contact with the heavy wood below, it's like an axe to my brain. I move faster, desperate to arrive at quiet—no more chopping, no more wailing, no more hearing crying in droplets of water or the swish of curtains.

The carrots are done. I plop them in the water, turn the dial, and the burner bursts to life with a whoosh of blue flame.

Do I have a few more minutes?

There is no wailing from upstairs.

I sit at the island, gulp my wine, then put my face in my hands. Granny Bea's needles click, clack, click, clack. Her chair rocks, banging on the hardwood floor of the parlor. But no, it's too loud. It doesn't sound like wood on wood. It's tile …

A small child giggles like chimes in the wind. Close, right in my ear.

I gasp and fly up from the island, sending my stool crashing to the floor. There is a flicker of movement in the corner of my eye and a small patter of feet in the other direction.

I try to ignore the children. I always try.

The pipes in the bathroom upstairs groan. The sound rushes over me like water, like the tub filling upstairs.

Mom is bathing him. That's good. Gives me more time. I pour myself another wine. We love this wine, Mom and I. The wine is there in empty spaces that need filled. We pick up cases every time we visit Fredericksburg. The families there are so large, their vineyards so lush, the wines so bold. Every sip of wine reminds me of road trips through the Hill Country, bluebonnets whispering in the breeze, laughter and cigarette smoke filling the empty expanse of our Oldsmobile Firenza.

Mom and I have already emptied a bottle, and it's only 7 p.m. I should slow down, but the alcohol muffles my endless, nagging responsibilities. The alcohol also heightens the small pleasures still available to me. The aroma of rosemary and sage steaming in the cavity of the fowl in the oven, the solid feel of the stamped concrete tile beneath my feet, the brilliance of the vast and lavish kitchen that spans around me like a cathedral.

I should consider myself lucky to be living in this house, handed down generation after generation. Hard to find old ranch land in the Hill Country now that won't cost you your first- born child. I should consider myself lucky that my husband decided to lube his cock with another woman's mouth so I could move home to my daddy's homestead with its sprawling land, many rooms, and a pool in which my child can swim when he gets older. I try to forget the trauma that lives here, as familiar to me as my own skin. The myriad skeletons in its many closets gave it a price tag befitting a single mother's budget.

My husband's philandering also left me with my pudge, extra wrinkles, and endless parenting responsibilities. He gets to screw, to party, to be a bachelor again, all while my vagina is still healing from the trauma of his spawn. But I guess I have this house, skeletons and all, which I both love and hate.

Steam billows from the pots on the stove. When I stir them, the damp air moistens my face, and I can taste the sweetness of the carrots and the earthy bite of the potatoes. Saliva pools beneath my tongue as I imagine mashing and mixing the veg with gravy. That had always been my favorite food—anything drowning in the gravy made with the secret family recipe. Among other things, that gravy recipe has been passed down for generations. I'll start the gravy while Mom is taking care of the bath, but she'll have to season it and thicken it just right. That art has not been passed down to me yet.

Remi's nails tick tick tick on the floor behind me. He's always under my feet when I'm cooking. Always barking when the baby needs to sleep. I love Remi, but sometimes he irritates the shit out of me. I want to not hear or feel anyone or anything, just for a solid half hour. I wait to feel his fur against my leg so I can scream at him to get out, but he must feel my mood. The ticking of his nails stops before he reaches me.

When I open the oven door, a blast of hot air blows my fine hair back from my face—the hair that isn't stuck to my cheeks by wine-induced sweat and vegetable steam, anyway. The scent of the poultry cooking in its juices is more intoxicating than the Cabernet. Donning an oven mitt, I tip the roaster just enough to get a ladle full of bird grease to mix with some flour, but when I bring it into the light, I notice something is wrong.

I pour the liquid into a saucepan. It is too thick. Too red. I tilt the pan back and forth, watching fingers of viscous fluid coat the pan, and I wonder how the chicken is still bleeding.

The pipes overhead groan, and something bangs and crashes. The baby is screeching and thrashing about in the tub like a feral beast. I marvel at how something so small can make such a damn ruckus. And such a mess. Grotesque diapers all day, that curdled yellow vomit after every feeding. And something so small, so soft, so pink, keeping me up night after night. Every minute, every second, wanting, needing, demanding …

Knock. Clack-click-clack. Knock. Clack-click-clack.

Granny Bea's incessant rocking and knitting, knitting and rocking is as bad as my boy's crying and shitting, puking, crying, shitting, sleepless hours upon hours …but the sound is too close. Granny Bea is in the parlor, knitting a jumper for her great-grandson, but the noise is here with me in the kitchen.

Knock. Click-clack-click.

I don't know what I'm expecting when I turn from the chicken-blood gravy on the stove, but it isn't to see Granny Bea sitting in her chair in the corner of the kitchen, rocking and knitting, knitting and rocking. Still, there she is.

"Gran?" Fear squeaks my voice out of my throat—a pinhole in a balloon.

Granny Bea's knitting needles tick together, gleaming like blades in the glare from the naked bulbs in the fixtures above. She is watching me, studying me, her eyes wide and dark.

With every rock, she licks her thick, dry tongue over her toothless gums, stretches her thin lips into a grin.

"Gran, how did you …"

The entrance, the hall, the parlor … it's quite a journey for someone who uses a cane.

For a woman who shuffles, not walks. A person with gout, arthritis and profound dementia.

Someone who can't move a can of soup, let alone an entire rocking chair. But here she is, knitting and rocking, staring and licking.

"Granny Bea, how on Earth did you get in here? You need to be careful!"

I go to her and check her over. I don't know if I expect to find a broken ankle, a laceration, a bruise. But Granny Bea seems perfectly intact and content. She is making exceptional progress on my son's jumper, except it's an absolute mess. She chose white yarn—worst color for anyone, let alone a baby—and it's covered in stains.

"Oh, Granny Bea," I say as I wipe at the half-constructed jumper with the sleeve of my hoodie.

But it isn't food. It's dark, and crumbly, and smears across the delicate ivory cotton when I rub it, staining it further.

Despite me tugging at the garment, Granny Bea's hands do not slow. She continues working away, pulling through stitch after stitch, her hands moving in robotic rhythm at a steady tempo. They are filthy. Black and mucky, with dirt packed in each wrinkle and fold.

"Gran, what have you been doing?"

I pull her hand to my face and sniff it. I don't know why I do that. Mothers do that, I guess, with unidentified stains and messes. I immediately regret my decision. The Cabernet burns my sinuses as it rushes back up my gorge, coerced out of digestion by the rancid stench of sick and rot.

"Granny Bea!" I shout as I recoil back against the island. "What have you gotten into?"

Granny Bea doesn't answer. She hasn't talked in years, not since she lost my grandfather in the accident. But she does make noise—grunts, giggles, mewls. And now she makes the most raucous, blood-curdling noise I've ever heard. She brays out laughter thick with mucus, and her folds and lumps jiggle in the chair as her whole body heaves. Remi howls behind me, just out of tune with Granny Bea's voice. He's right behind me, and so loud, and Granny Bea's so gross, and the thrashing in the tub upstairs is getting louder, so loud that I drop to the floor and cover my ears, close my eyes.

The unpleasant noise stops. All of it. No more howling, rocking, no click-clacking of knitting needles, no more laughter thick with the fluids of death. I allow my hands to drop from my ears. The kitchen is filled with the gentle gurgling of boiling water and the soft whir of the oven.

I open my eyes and see shoes. Two pairs of shoes, shiny black. Freshly polished.

I sit up, let my eyes rise to see two pairs of pants, side-by-side, two white button-down shirts with ducks embroidered on the collars. And two sets of milky white eyes buried in pallid, translucent skin.

I've seen these boys before. Always running around my goddamn kitchen. They can't be more than five or six. Twins, towheaded, with black lips and necrotic fingertips. I reach out to them like they are my own sons, and they reach back, their faces contorted in fear, in horror, in pain. When they open their mouths to scream, I hear it, and it is my son's wails. That sound is impossible, though, because no air can pass out of these boys. Wet dirt erupts from their mouths, vomiting down their tidy, pressed clothes. Dirt is coming from everywhere—their ears, their eyes, soiling both the fronts and backs of their trousers. I scream, they scream, and dirt shoots so forcefully from their faces that it splits their heads in two. The four skull halves fall to the floor, and masses of worms slither out, chasing me, crawling up my legs, into every orifice, and still, still my son screams in pain from the mouths of these boys.

"Darling?"

The boys are gone.

There were never any boys. Not here, not in this house.

I hate this house.

"What?" I snap at my mom, who is standing in the entrance to the kitchen.

I shoot a glance at the corner where Granny Bea had been rocking. She is still rocking, but not there. I hear her down the hall, the wood of her chair knocking the wood of the parlor floor. I look where the twins had been standing. I wildly scour the kitchen but find only boiling pots on the stove and an empty wine bottle on the island.

"You drink too much," my mom dares to say.

I know this.

"There is nothing wrong with me," I snark, mimicking her.

Mom nods and looks down her nose.

There is so much wrong with both of us.

"I'm sorry about dinner," Mom says, her trembling hand motioning to the pots on the stove. "Again."

"Shit." I forgot the food.

The potatoes and carrots are fine, but the bloody grease is smoldering. I look inside. The liquid, now black and smoking, is full of hair. But not my hair, pale and long. Short, coarse hair.

Dog hair.

I pull the saucepan off and toss it in the sink. It clatters, but not like metal on metal. It sounds like someone emptied a sack of bones into the sink. I don't dare look to see if that's true.

"Another wine?" Mom asks.

She's already stabbed the corkscrew into a vintage bottle.

"I thought you said I drink too much."

She nods. "We do what we have to."

Mom is a blank woman. Her face is empty, her mouth a tight, thin line. As her hands turn, pulling out the cork, I try to remember those hands on my body. She was never much of a hugger. She didn't braid my hair or hold my hand. I wonder, as I have many times, if Granny Bea ever brushed Mom's hair, or rubbed her back when she was sick, or kissed her on the forehead. I have never seen affection between the two. But Granny Bea had been sick for quite some time. I only remember cold, silence, rigid indifference. From both of them. From all of us.

Am I cold to my son too?

I should check the chicken, but I don't want to. I bend, look through the stained, yellowed window of the oven at the meat. It's steaming, the meat bursting and sizzling, Remi's tongue lolling over the side of the roaster.

I gasp. Stumble back and look to my mom as if she's going to help me. She is drinking wine from her perch at the island, with Remi by her side. His head is on her lap, but she is not petting him like she always does. He nudges her with his snout, but she doesn't react. Instead, she reacts to me, her gaze settling on my face.

I turn back around and stand overtop of the stove, steam billowing in my face, my mom's cold stare piercing my back.

"You are tired," she says.

It's more than tired.

"It's hard," I say.

"What's hard?"

Everything.

"I'm tired," I echo.

Something beside the island moves. I steal a peek. It is a little boy, chocolate eyes and hair the color of the peaches in the fruit basket on the counter. Hair not unlike my own, but his isn't thin and scraggly from the hormones of childbirth and breastfeeding. He has time to wash and brush his hair, a luxury I don't have with a babe always pawing at me, screaming, suckling at my teat.

"A mother's work is never done," Mom says behind me, punctuating her wisdom with a sip of her wine.

I cannot take my eyes off the boy child. He is singing a familiar melody, something trapped in the shadows of my brain, words I can't quite understand or remember. He smiles, and I gasp. His teeth are rotted and sharp, and his tongue is a worm, writhing as it's pierced over and over again by the child's sharp incisors as his jaw moves with song.

"Mom?" I ask without forming an actual question.

Mom peers over the island. Her eyes linger a moment on the boy, then she directs her attention back to the wine, filling the two glasses fuller than a proper wine should be poured.

More than we should be having before the dinner is even served. From the other room, I hear Granny Bea's rocking, hear the click-clack-click of those knitting needles. I refuse to look at the little ginger boy any longer, and I need a distraction from the noise of Granny Bea, so I direct my attention back to the pots on the stove. The ones that don't need me.

"Sit," Mom says. She is not asking.

And though I do like a good argument with my mother, I choose to be agreeable. Not to appease her but because I am weary. It feels like my legs might give out at any moment.

"Being a mom is hard," she says.

I take one, two, three gulps of my wine. I cannot help but take offense to her burnout. It's the labor of me she's referring to. The young me, who needed fed, who refused to go to bed on time. Who bit a girl on a playdate so was uninvited to the rest, leaving her mother isolated and bored. Who pitched fits in stores and slammed doors when she was upset about boundaries and rules.

I wonder if I'll resent my son the way my mom resents me.

"Do you hate it?" I ask.

"Hate what?"

"Being a mom."

Her eyes widen as if she's just received a dagger between the ribs.

"I love you," she says.

I know that. Love was never the question.

"Yes, but, besides me … do you love being a mom?"

Mom's mouth moves as if she's chewing on the answer, rolling it around her tongue to find something palatable to swallow.

"No," she says.

The word strikes me like a slap.

"Do you wish you'd never had me?" I ask.

"I wish I'd never lost myself."

Neither of us acknowledge the tears glistening on each other's cheeks. I don't bother to wipe mine away. I let them drip into my wine glass.

Everything is loud again. The gurgling of the boiling on the stove, the knock of Granny Bea's chair. There is movement in the corner, and I try not to look, I try so hard, but I know she's back. Somehow, Granny Bea is back, sitting in that corner, hands covered in rot, knitting and rocking, rotting and knitting.

Something brushes my pant leg. I look down at my feet and find the little ginger boy skittering past, moving like an animal on his hands and feet toward the corner, forcing me to look. Granny Bea is there, in her rocker, in worse shape than she was before. Her hands are black with dirt, and her eye sockets are full of worms. She is naked and splayed out, the sheen of fresh childbirth glistening between her legs. The twin boys are there too, one attached to each of her breasts, suckling, slurping.

Mom sees too, but her mouth is not agape in horror. She can breathe, can lift her wineglass without trembling.

"Why are they here?" I ask. "Granny Bea and the twins. This is my house."

"Our house," Mom reminds me.

Granny Bea had been haunted. I could tell by the way she used to watch the corners, smile at silent jokes, shield her eyes from unknown terrors. I never knew the twins. Mom's brothers. They were gone so very young.

"You know, having kids took so much from me," Mom says. "It wasn't your fault, of course. I gave myself willingly. But we only have so much to give, us mothers. Only so much."

Her words sting.

"Was it ever good?"

"Oh yes. Many good moments. But the bad moments encase you in a caul, preventing you from seeing anything but the repetition, the struggle, the isolation. Eventually, all the good moments turn sour because they, too, are encased, all part of the same stew that roils you over and over again, day after day."

Panic starts to take hold. That happens more and more lately. The racing heart, the need to run, to get away, like my organs are splintering, my mind is fracturing, and the sky might compress me into the dirt.

"Please tell me it gets better," I plead.

I am sobbing. She is not. Her head tilts, and I think she's judging me.

"What do I do?" I cry. "I need help. I need …"

I don't know what I need. I don't even know what I want. Do I want to be free again? Do I want my husband back, someone to help share the workload? Or do I want to be less broken?

The perfect mother who glows, and who enriches their child at every moment and cherishes each and every milestone, hiccup, breath.

The ginger boy crab crawls up onto the island. His legs and arms are bent at odd angles, and his head is propped sideways on his shoulders, not quite squared with the rest of his body.

He is broken but smiling a jagged, sharp smile, blissfully unaware of his condition. He plays with the fruit bowl, humming his lullaby, rolling an orange back and forth until Mom picks it up in her hand. He stops, his eyes narrow to slits, and his song ceases, replaced by a feral growl from deep in his belly. He launches at Mom, his sharp teeth bared, but Gran heaves to her feet.

She scoops the ginger boy up under her arm and hauls him off into the house as he thrashes and howls. Mom pierces the orange with her nails, and juice dribbles onto the counter.

"We mothers have to stick together," she says, looking down the hall that swallowed Granny. "Your grandmother helped me."

Wait …

"What did you say?" I ask.

"Hmmm?"

"Before. You said having kids took so much from you."

"Indeed," Mom says. "As it does all mothers."

I lean forward, forcing her to look in my eyes.

"Kids," I say.

"Kids?"

"You said kids. Not kid. Kids."

I stare into her eyes, and she stares into mine. She is trying to see my thoughts. I'm trying to figure out what it is I think I've realized.

Mom stands and goes to the stove. She picks up a spoon and stirs the water. She is disgusted, afraid, something.

"I can help you," Mom says. "Just like Granny Bea helped me."

"Who is the boy?" I ask.

Mom stops stirring. Her eyes are transfixed on the pot and the contents within.

Her voice is a bullet. "Your brother."

My heart clenches. "I don't have a brother."

Mom keeps looking at the pot. Stirring.

"You don't," she agrees. "Anymore."

In the other room, the rocking ignites, and the giggle of children fills the halls.

"You know," Mom says, and the corner of her mouth twitches into a smile. "Your grandmother and I loved gardening. We used to garden so much. The fresh vegetables for us to cook every night were glorious. You could just taste the soil churned by our hands. The life we planted there."

The rocking is oh so loud again, and Mom's voice is growing softer. I stand from the island, wobble, my legs weak from wine and fear and exhaustion. I go to Mom, to the stove, because I can't hear her over Granny Bea and the children.

"This house," Mom says. "Such a lavish, grand monster of a thing. Just look at this kitchen! The kitchen was always my favorite. Gran's too. All the dishes we'd make. When you're cooking, creating, there's no room in the mind for anything else."

The children bound through the kitchen naked, smeared with dirt—the two blond boys with leafy greens staining their hair and the ginger boy with aphids for freckles.

"I had a brother?" I am sobbing, shaking.

Mom nods.

Granny Bea is back, rocking in the corner of the kitchen, the twins latched back onto her pie plate nipples.

"My brothers were needy, squalling things, just like yours was," Mom says.

I don't want to look. But I have to, even though I already know. I go to Mom. Look in the pot. It isn't carrots. It's fingers, an entire pot full, decayed and bloated, maggots writhing under tiny yellowed nails. And in the potato pot, tiny stomachs, heads, hearts.

"I didn't hate your brother, like your grandmother didn't hate mine. We just …"

Granny Bea's jaw drops open, and an awful keen explodes out of her mouth. And the three boys scream too. It is the sound of lambs at slaughter—pain, desperation, panic.

"Here," Mom says as she hands me a spoon. "Stir. It's soothing."

I stir.

All the crying from all the mouths withers until it is nothing more than the soft sound of boiling water.

I am startled as something falls down the stairs in a dozen heavy thuds. Then movement echoes through the hall—a sliding, dragging sound. Slow, clumsy.

I look away from the fingers in the pot, over the island, to the hall beyond. There is a shape there, a blob, pale and blue and bloated, struggling toward the kitchen.

"Where?" I mumble.

"You are tired," Mom says. "But you don't have to be."

"Where is he?"

"Being a mom doesn't have to be a life sentence, you know."

Mom sits at the island and pours another glass of wine.

"They're never really gone," Mom says. "Every time I peel a potato, cut a stalk of celery, dice an onion … Our babies are dirt beneath our nails that we'll never be rid of. Reminders of what we planted, what we grew."

"Did you leave him in the bath?"

Mom pours wine in my glass.

"You know … you have a beautiful garden outside."

Upstairs, my son screams. Gurgles. His voice is becoming slower, weaker …

In the kitchen, the twins suckle at Granny Bea's eternally full breasts as my brother steers hot wheels around the grout roads on the tile floor.

Granny Bea rocks and knits. Mom hums the lullaby with my brother, a dissonant duet. I take a long draw of my wine, savoring the taste of road trips and laughter and happiness long passed, as the music of the bathwater upstairs decrescendos to silence.

THE DISAPPEARING WOMEN

By Carmen Gray

MONICA'S LIPS WERE SLICK WITH red lipstick as she read the teleprompter's words to the screen. "Don't forget, it's Wife Day and there's all kinds of wonderful events for finding that perfect mate. Our great governor reminds us that it's patriotic to make partnerships on one of our favorite national holidays and generously offers a free three-course meal at one of his participating restaurants around our beautiful state of Texas." She smiled broadly. The girl-next-door look that boosted ratings for the network had worked in her favor for three years now.

She herself was pursued by multiple male colleagues in their late fifties, but was holding out because she didn't want to give up her career to become a wife and a mother just yet. But she knew she couldn't fend off the inevitable much longer. There was a new, younger blonde who her boss recently hired to help her last month, even though she had coyly pleaded that she didn't need Ashley. And she suspected Ashley was real, unlike herself. But the unspoken truth was that she had been just like Ashley once upon a time and eventually replaced Julie, the former anchorwoman who came of age, too.

No woman got past the age of twenty-seven without becoming wed if they knew what was good for them. And even if they didn't and made the mistake that Monica was told to report about on the five o'clock news, at least they could be matched as well. There were lonely, single men who couldn't find a wife of their own volition and they were willing to forego the purity search to be matched to avoid the high taxes imposed on single males who didn't enlist. So it really wasn't much of a choice at all. Find a decent mate and perhaps even romance before it was all decided for you.

Josh walked by after she went off air and leaned in close enough for Monica to smell his sour breath. If only she could have stuck with Julio right out of college. But Julio didn't have the choices she had. The government needed young men for the military. That way, there were enough young women available to marry the older men. It was a good plan. They got the biggest tax breaks. The ones whose wives had withered away from the "diseases" that seemed to come up every so often. Men like Josh had access to resources and likely still had possessions that had not been confiscated from the raids. Like her boss. His wife was Monica's age and already pregnant with their second child. She seemed like she had a good life. She even bragged about having a nanny, which was rare these days since all of the immigrants had been banned from the state. Julio had even nearly been taken, despite, like her, being from a long line of native Texans. He had the wrong color of skin. Thank goodness he agreed to enlist to avoid…being sent who knows where. Josh cleared his throat, bringing her back to the present moment. She suppressed a knot in her stomach when he spoke.

"Well, I think it's high time we finally go out, don't you?" He cast a furtive glance in her direction, his eyes lingering on her chest. She instinctively covered herself with her hand, but he took it in his and gave it a warm squeeze. Studying his face while he held her hand, she imagined that once upon a time he had probably been handsome, maybe even like Julio, only with lighter skin. She could just go out with him and try to imagine Julio's face instead of his. Conjuring up Julio's image, she could envision his beautiful, smooth face in place of the crinkles that formed around Josh's hooded eyes and a youthful jawline that didn't sag. She sighed as she glanced at the extra fat gathered under Josh's chin, but she knew that her boss would approve. And so would her audience at home who watched the news faithfully. That's what they all wanted. It would help boost the ratings. Soon enough, Ashley would have her job and Monica wouldn't have a choice anyways. She should just accept the offer. So she did.

Monica expected Josh to take her to Taste of Texas, the restaurant sponsored by the governor, but he had other plans. He drove her to his place, a high rise decked in mid-century modern furniture that overlooked the river that wound through the city. It was impressive, but she tried to keep her expression from revealing too much. Few people had such luxuries these days. Most lived in small housing projects, not unlike the place Monica had been afforded while she worked at the network. She surveyed the collection of fine wine inside a beautiful maple cabinet. Beside it, a bookshelf caught her eye. Since the libraries had been shuttered, there were few, if any books available at the state stores and most of them were written by the same handful of authors on the same few subjects and all were only available in English. There were the ones she had saved that she kept hidden in a box under her bed. Ones that she knew were forbidden. Like La Selva, the Spanish translation of Upton Sinclair's banned book that her aunt had left her before disappearing. She could only remember a few phrases in Spanish anymore and had certainly been careful to hide that fact.

"Like what you see? It could all be yours in a heartbeat. You have no idea how much I have to offer you," Josh said, following her gaze. She forced herself to smile as he continued. "Listen, Monica, you're on the brink of letting yourself go. I've seen it happen before with other young women your age. Not a good path," he scolded, pouring her a glass of vintage wine as he arched an eyebrow at her. "You're lucky I find you attractive. I could have anyone. But I like you." He paused, then touched her hair. She forced herself not to flinch. "I know you bleach it. I know you're a fake. But I still like you."

Her heart fluttered wildly inside her chest. She had gotten too comfortable lately and she knew better. Fabiola had warned her. "If you get tired of the hair treatments, I know someone who makes wigs out of real hair. Just shave your head, like the Egyptians did and wear one." But Monica wondered where this person was getting blonde hair? It was in high demand. Josh brushed a lock of her hair behind her ear. She could feel his eyes burning into her, begging her to meet his. She kept her gaze downcast, looking at the peek-a-boo kitten heels she was required to wear for work. She wished she was at home, wearing her soft pajamas and fluffy slippers.

Josh tipped her chin up to force her to look at him. She stared at his salt-and-pepper hair. His broad shoulders seemed to tower over her as he leaned down to breathe into her ear, "I've been so patient. I've waited a long time for you, but you've brushed off my advances." He pressed himself into her. "I'm what you call an acquired taste. Give me a chance. I could make you happy." She squeezed her eyes shut, trying to imagine Julio this close to her instead of Josh, but it wouldn't work. Julio had been gentle and what they had seemed like a nascent love affair from a million years ago.

A tart aroma wafted to her nose. She opened her eyes as Josh raised the glass of wine to her lips. She kept them tightly shut, her jaw beginning to twitch. She feigned laughter to lighten the mood. Wasn't that what men liked? How was she going to get out of this situation now? She knew it wasn't safe to lower her inhibitions around anyone. Isn't that how some of the women she heard about in the newsroom got into bad situations that led to their demise? Just ten more years and this era of coerced marriages would be over. That's when the resources wouldn't be so scarce anymore. Like good food and clean water. And books. And good wine. She had a bottle stashed at her house that a married friend had snuck her a few weeks ago. But she only took a few sips by herself to be safe. In fact, the last time she had it was on her porch with her dog, Chispa. She enjoyed her alone time in her own space, provided by the network. She loved painting pictures of the sunset in the company of her beloved German Shepherd with no one to pressure her or make her feel like time was running out for living alone and she knew she was privileged to have her own place these days. Being loyal to the state had its perks.

Josh opened her lips with his thumb and index finger, pouring the velvety liquid into her mouth. A little bit dribbled down her chin. He stuck out his tongue, the tip of it flicking it off of her, like a toad searching for a fly. Chills moved down her spine as she glanced over at the shelf behind him. There were pictures of him with a woman and a girl. He looked much younger in the photo, his hair and eyebrows darker, not a speck of gray in them. But the woman next to him looked just like her.

"Is that you?" Monica asked, hoping to distract him.

"What's that?" Josh asked, setting down the glass so he could fondle her breasts with both of his hands. Her back stiffened as she asked him about the photo again. He glanced over at the photo and stopped groping her momentarily. Relieved, she took the opportunity to step away from him.

"Oh, yes, that's me. That was my wife and daughter," he murmured.

Monica studied the photo more, looking at the round eyes of the little girl. She found herself deeply envious. She looked like any of the young girls that attended the elementary school across the street from her house. If only she had been born when those children were. This generation would have it so much easier than hers when they came of age. Everything had changed when Monica was eight. Just long enough to have seen a very different kind of life for women. Like her Tía Maria, who went from living contentedly on her own in Houston as an immigration attorney to disappearing when she refused to marry after her job was deleted. Her mother told her it was due to an epidemic that year, a virus that broke out that affected mostly women. But Monica had seen the memos left carelessly about the newsroom these days. There were no viruses. She just had to say there were. And now she was about to be swallowed up by this devil of a man who was old enough to be her father or she might disappear, like his wife must have. Like her Tía. Like so many others.

"You're stunning," Josh said, his fingers sliding into her shirt. "I fell in love with Jani when she was your age. Jani could only give me one child, but I think you'll bear more children, especially with these hips," he moved his hands up and down her body. "Men can spread their seed until they die. We have a duty to do so, you know."

Monica wondered what it would be like to not run out of time. She closed her eyes to escape where she was now. Just like she did when she reported the news each day. An image of her childhood friend flashed in her mind. Fabiola had stopped by the station last month. When she delivered secret information about yet another directive from the state, her amber eyes held concern in them. Monica asked her if everything would be okay.

"Not for me, Monica. I won't be able to teach anymore. Time is up." She snapped her fingers and looked at Monica in disbelief. "I'm here to tell you that all of the female teachers will be fired. But the official statement I have to give you to report is that the state is matching husbands for all of us so that we don't have to work anymore. That it is a generous move." She drew in her breath and cast a glance around the room to ensure that they were still alone. "But that's not the truth, Monica. The truth is we know too much and therefore we are dangerous. I have to leave before I disappear."

At the time Monica had laughed, thinking it couldn't be true. When Fabiola stared blankly back at her reaction, an inkling of fear creeped into her.

"You know it's not a virus, even though you report that it is, right? Maybe one day you'll be brave enough to report what's really happening out there," Fabiola hissed at her. "You could save lives. I've told you that before."

Monica was unsure of how to respond. No one dared defy orders. She knew the truth was that if she did, she might end up like Tía Maria, all those years ago. She was happy with her dog and her little place where she could be alone for now. It had been so easy to just follow the script. Now the expectation was to marry Josh or any of the many suitors. She was lucky, wasn't she? Many women didn't even have the ability she had to live out her life without any troubles. But, would it be easy, really? Now, with Josh slobbering over her, she wondered if she could be okay with being a wife. She felt nothing for him but contempt at the moment. And she was still haunted by the last thing Fabiola told her.

"Look, I can see you are curious, but doubtful. I thought I would be one of the safe ones, too. But none of us is safe without a husband. And even after you get one, once you have raised the allotted children, you won't be safe anymore. They'll disappear you to one of those places where they do experiments on women because you won't be of any use to society anymore. But, there's an out. You can call me." Fabiola handed her a number on a piece of paper. "It can't be traced." Monica still had the number in her purse. All she had to do was make that call. Was it too late?

Josh's rancid breath blew into Monica's face as he pulled her skirt down past her thighs. He rubbed against her through his clothes. "Be my wife," he said, his voice ragged. Monica stared into the picture of him with his former wife, who looked like her and his daughter as he began to unzip his pants. "You're a good girl," he said, opening her legs with his knees. She had never slept with a man his age before. In fact, she had only ever been with Julio and Josh could never ever know that. They had messed around, but they had been very careful and she had only let him enter her once while she was on her period. It was dangerous enough that they got that far, not to mention that if he told anyone about it, it would have ruined her career and her chance to marry someone like…Josh. But she knew Julio would never have done that. "Amor," he had told her, "Tenemos un secreto eternal." We have an eternal secret. And part of that was their shared language. Where was Julio now? She wondered. Off fighting some curated war in another attempted land grab somewhere? Or dead? Who knew. She had to let go of any notion that she would ever see him again in this life. It was interfering with her ability to acquiesce to her duty now.

As Josh went in for a kiss, it felt as though he was attempting to consume her completely with his mouth. It was not romantic or gentle. His tongue was one big tentacle, like a slimy independent creature, searching for something hidden in her. She held in a gag and pushed him away.

"I'm sorry, I think I must be sick from something I ate at lunch today," Monica lied, hoping it would keep him at bay. But he took it as a challenge as he lunged at her, pinning her against the wall.

"Oh, I know this game and it turns me on. I get bored easily, you know. I like this kind of play," he said as he pushed her to the ground. She slid down the wall, horrified at how Josh had transformed from casual co-worker to monster in private.

"Kneel, baby," he ordered her as he started to unzip his trousers. Monica's heart raced inside her chest. What would happen if she did not obey? Her little place, her sanctuary with her dog and her paints and the hidden books and her fantasies about a different life with Julio still existed. But not for long. She could see Fabiola's number on the scrap of paper in her mind.

"Be a good girl, now and just give it a lick. Then I'll give you the ring of your dreams and make you a proper wife."

Monica's feet hurt inside her shoes. She felt for the sharp edge of the heel. They were pretty and also the most uncomfortable ones she owned. She glanced up, noticing how low Josh's balls hung. They reminded her of an old goat.

"Okay," she purred at Josh. "Close your eyes so you can really enjoy it." He smiled down at her, his jowls shaking as he laughed. "Oh, I knew you'd be a good girl," he said, "I know all about you. I know you're not really pure. But, you're lucky. I'll still make you a good wife," he smiled as he closed his eyes. How did he know about her private life? She panicked as he reached a hand to place behind her head in order to mash her face into him, but she played the game well and ducked, his hand swinging at the air in vain. And before he knew it, the sharp point of a heel slammed into his balls, stunning him as he stumbled backwards, his face contorted in both surprise and pain.

"What the actual fuck? You idiotic bitch! You're over. Do you realize that??" He sat, crumpled up with his pants halfway down his legs, looking more vulnerable than Monica could have ever imagined. He attempted to get back up, but there was a lot of blood coming from where she struck him. By the time he looked up, she had fled his place.

Monica gasped for air as she bolted from the apartment and down the hall toward the elevators, holding the blessed shoe in her right hand. She tripped and fell in her haste. A couple, not unlike Josh and herself would have looked, approached her, the woman with a genuine look of concern on her face.

"Oh my goodness. Everything okay?" She asked as she reached out a hand to pull Monica back up to standing. Monica brushed her hair out of her face, still holding the weapon in her hand.

"Aren't you Monica from the news? We just love you!" The young woman exclaimed. Then she glanced down and grimaced. Monica followed her gaze to the shoe she held, with blood on the heel.

"Sorry, I'm late for an appointment," Monica blurted out as she turned and rushed toward the elevators. The doors were closing. There was a sound at the end of the hallway, but she didn't dare turn around now. She was almost there. And then she could call Fabiola.

"Grab her, she assaulted me!" Josh's voice echoed down the hall. The sound of feet hitting the ground came closer as she reached the elevator doors, which were now closed. Was it too late? Had she missed her chance?

"Miss. Monica!" a voice shouted. It was the woman. Monica turned around in horror as the woman, young and fit and fertile like herself, approached her. Was there a chance that she would help her? Would she understand? She searched the woman's face for some kind of sign of mutual understanding.

"Call the police!" Josh's voice boomed loudly again.

But the woman's eyes were hollow as she grabbed Monica's arm. Her husband was on his phone, down the hallway, standing by Josh at his door.

"Help me," Monica mouthed to the woman. She cocked her head to the side, like a puppy.

"What do you mean?" the woman said, her grasp on Monica's arm unyielding. Monica noticed how taut her skin was, so dewy and bright. Her blonde hair cascaded over her shoulders in soft, shimmering waves. Did she have to bleach it like Monica? Her ice blue eyes blinked mechanically.

"They're going to disappear me," Monica yelped helplessly at the woman, who released her quickly.

"Are you ill? Don't tell me you caught the virus!?" The woman shrank back in horror. Monica realized this was her chance to run, but it was too late. The elevator doors opened. A pair of policemen arrived, ready to take her away to the place she knew about but never dared report about on the news. She tried to scream, but nothing came out of her mouth. Her voice had all but disappeared.

THIS I KNOW

By Iphigenia Strangeworth

Zilpah

THE MAN AND THE GIRL aren't related, but they both had blue eyes when Mordecai brought them home. Hers are fake, though, color contact lenses-an alteration of her God-given body, a sin in the sight of the Lord. Her hair is bleached blonde, her face painted like a whore, her nose pierced like a bull's, and she has tattoos, a circle on a cross between her breasts, a cross on her ring finger, a red rose on her thigh, and, most interesting, a black snake tied in a strange knot low on her torso.

"What is it?" I ask her quietly, pointing to the snake. She tries to lunge forward, screams when the chains catch her and dig into her wrists, her ankles, her neck. The man has learned by now that struggling against the chains won't get him anywhere, but the girl is still wild. "What is it?"

"A cottonmouth," the girl finally snaps, her lips pulled back in imitation of the snake on her belly.

"The shape, what is it?"

"Uterus."

"'You shall not make any cuts on your body for the dead or tattoo yourselves; I am the *Lord.*'" Daddy always reads it like that, "the *Lord*".

"Bible contradicts itself everywhere," the girl grunts, "and God didn't write it, anyway, men did. A whole bunch of men with different ideas. If Jesus didn't say it, I ain't readin' it."

"You're going to Hell."

"'Thou shalt not kill,'" the girl says, eyes bright with fever and fire and pure, desperate hatred, "I know that. Ain't you ever heard that, huh?"

"You're going to Hell," I repeat.

"I'll meet you there," she hisses.

I've never been allowed to feed the sinners before. I've never been around them during their punishment at all, between the time Mordecai brings them home and the slaughter. Daddy says they're all the same underneath, and maybe it's only because they're so new to me, but these two seem different, more human. Hagar agrees with me to a certain extent; she says all the sinners have their quirks, confessed that she gives them nicknames to tell them apart. The last three were Adulteress, Cuckold and Bastard; these two are Harlot and Sodomite. It's not friendship if I call them by their crimes, just a way to tell them apart from the others.

I helped with the slaughters of the last three, which, according to Daddy, means I can finally be more fully involved with the sinners. He kills them, of course- always- but I watched my brother, Mordecai, process the carcasses, and I skinned part of Bastard's arm for practice, flushed and scraped his intestines, skinned his legs and cut the meat into sections, put everything in the deep freezer. I did all the cooking, too, since Nana has no hands and Hagar wants me to be more involved. *You'll be a better wife if you learn this now, Zilpah. You don't want to end up like me, do you? Unmarried?*

I'm not much better looking than her, honestly, but my face is more even. Her left eye is much higher than her right, and her mouth is sort of tilted, like God was distracted when He assembled my big sister's face. Hagar is ugly, but she's *so* smart, and Zilthai, my twin, is blind, deaf and dumb, but she's the prettiest of us all. Mordecai says he loves us both- me for my excellent cooking and feminine nature, Zilthai for her beauty. Mordecai has always liked women more than men. He says women are kinder, simpler, far more lovely, and, of course, we taste better. Hagar doesn't believe him. *He just likes feeling smart,* she sneered when I asked her about him, *and he only gets to feel smart with you and Zilthai. Notice how he ignores Nana and I.*

Hagar is probably jealous that Mordecai wants me, but I've never said that to her face. I never want to hurt my sister; Daddy says she's a *woman of boundless virtue.* If the girl in the barn, Harlot, the whore with snake eyes to match her cottonmouth tattoo, was more like Hagar, she wouldn't be chained up out there, waiting to die.

"'There is nothing, nothing, I tell you, that keeps wicked men at any one moment out of Hell, but the mere pleasure of God,'" Daddy yells, and I stare out the window towards the barn, unable to listen and focus on him at the same time. He was a Southern Baptist preacher before he took Mama and Nana away from the sin and corruption of the outside world, and he still loves to preach, fire and brimstone sermons he wrote for his congregation years ago. Zilthai pokes her fingers into her empty eye sockets, tracing circles, and I absentmindedly reach to pat her head. She twists to bite my hand at once, nearly draws blood before I manage to pull it away.

Every night, we have to sit and listen to Daddy's sermons. I love them, I love his passion, but it gets kind of old, sitting and listening to a speech you've heard a million times before. I wonder why he doesn't bother to write new material. By the time we're excused, my legs are falling asleep and Zilthai is eating the skin off her lips. Mordecai puts a hand between her shoulders to guide her upstairs, but she drops to all fours, crawls away so fast she might as well be sprinting, and vanishes out the back door.

"She'll be fine," I say. Zilthai knows her way in the dark better than anyone.

Zilthai

The sinners are always kept in the barn, and I always know when new ones arrive, when the air stinks of fear, bodily waste and vomit, and something else, indescribable, an undercurrent no one else can pick up on. When I lost my eyes, I thought I might as well roll over and die, but in the six years since then I've learned to move through the world on all fours or with my arms outstretched, my nose pricked up, my tongue lolling out. I make better use of my three remaining senses than anyone else does with their five. Hagar keeps me away from the sinners when they first arrive; I must make us look bad, trying to get to know them.

I guess no one knew she was bringing this girl back, though, because I felt it the second she stepped foot in our house, her unfamiliar tread on the worn floorboards, ran to her before anyone could drag me to my room and grabbed her by the hair to feel her face, sniff behind her ears, lick her neck. It was Hagar who pulled me back, Nana who slapped me, and Zilpah who took me upstairs, because Hagar doesn't want her around, either, if she can help it. I vaguely remember Hagar's face, twisted enough to be considered pretty deformed, but being ugly isn't a crime. An ugly woman, on her own, isn't enough to raise suspicion. A deformed woman, a feral girl with no eyes, and a half-wit girl who just sits and stares are enough to give anyone pause.

This new girl, the one I got ahold of, is different from the last batch, different from the man. They're kept right next to each other, both of them chained to the concrete floor, both of them naked. Daddy and Mordecai maintain the restraints, ensure they'll never escape, so I'm not scared to approach them, touch them, smell them and lick at their sweaty skin. The man has been here a week, the girl two days, and he's calmed down enough that I think I can ask for his name. Hagar used to call them by their sin; I don't know if she still does.

As usual, the stench makes my stomach jolt as soon as I walk in, an impossibly thick combination of blood and waste and that ever-present fear, and I pause to gag before making my way to the man's enclosure. The enclosures used to be horse stalls, so I crawl over the gate instead of opening it- I don't have the padlock key- and smell his fear sharpen as I approach. Hagar used to hose them down every morning and evening, but Zilpah does it now, my sweet, impressionable, murderously innocent twin, and she's an idiot, so I already know she must have done it wrong. Sure enough, when I force the man's legs apart and lick his inner thigh, he tastes of old urine and dried feces, he must have a rash- so the girl, who was menstruating when we brought her here, has to be even worse off. The chains should be longer, long enough for them to relieve themselves in a corner, but I know it's deliberate, Daddy relishes their humiliation at being forced to soil themselves. The chains are tight and short enough that they can't move from their kneeling position, always on their knees, hands bound behind their backs.

I can feel the man shaking, reach up to touch his face, his tears, and slowly, gently, bring my hand to his chest. He's breathing so rapidly I'm scared he'll faint, I feel his rabbit-fast heartbeat against my palm and pause to take in as much of him as I can, his sparse chest hair, his prominent ribs. He doesn't calm down, so I go ahead and trace the letters, *N-A-M-E*. It's always been forbidden to humanize the sinners, but I'll do what I want. The day God comes down from His throne to bless Daddy is the day I'll believe in the righteousness of his cause.

The man doesn't react, so I repeat it, reach behind his back so he can trace letters onto my palm, do it again and again until he shakily copies me. *N-A-M-E.* I shake my head, snap my teeth and jerk forward suddenly just to feel him lean away, poke him in the chest and trace *N-A-M-E* again. Finally, he seems to understand, traces out his name, *C-L-E-M-E-N-T.* I pat his cheek, run my fingers over the stubble on his sharp jaw. He hasn't grown much of a beard. I tap my own chest, then reach out and write *Z-I-L-T-H-A-I.* I tell them all my name. Once the girl calms down, I'll exchange names with her, too.

I have to repeat myself several times before he traces my name back to me. *Z-I-L-T-H-A-I.* He knows me, now, and I know him. The last man was named John, his wife was Emilia, and their son was Cal. Before that, it was Gertrude; before her, Marcus and Dustin; before them, Diane; before her, Avery, and so on, for years and years and years. There've been families before, duos or trios of friends, but never two strangers. In the past, Daddy has always waited a few months, at least, before sending Mordecai out to find another hitchhiker or broken-down minivan or drunkard stumbling in the street. Until all the leather is tanned and the meat's run out. I wonder why we've got two, now, two who came in separately.

Clement nudges me, suddenly, rather awkwardly, and I stretch behind him again, put my palm where he can reach it. His hands are trembling, it takes several lengthy tries, but finally he writes *H-E-L-P M-E,* and I pull away, snarling. What does he expect me to do for him? Let him out, when

I don't even know where the keys are? And where would he go if I did? We're at least a hundred miles from the nearest town- he'd have better luck hoping to reach the road, but even if he did, my family would find him again before anyone else. It's all backroads here, no highway, no neighbors, no one to hear him scream for miles around. Besides, I doubt anyone would be willing to help a panicked, naked man, covered in his own blood and shit and rambling about monsters in the woods. I want to ask if he'd let someone like that into his car, driving alone or with his family in the middle of nowhere. It sounds like a horror movie, some crazy man screaming about evil hillbillies in rural Texas.

I can feel him trembling again, touch his shoulders and find them shaking with the force of his broken sobs. His face is wet with tears, and I chew my bloody, painfully chapped lower lip, lean forward carefully to hug him. Clement tenses up, his chest heaves, and I wonder if he'll throw up on me- he wouldn't be the first- but then he relaxes, leans into my embrace. He was skinny when he got here, and he's already starting to lose weight; there's never as much meat as you'd expect, and it's never good quality. The beef Daddy brings home from his twice-a-month trips into town always tastes better, but he believes it's a sin to waste anything. What we can't eat, Hagar turns into jewelry, leather, or decoration.

I have no way of knowing exactly how old Clement is. He has body hair, a more prominent Adam's apple than a boy, so he must be an adult, and he isn't so old that I can feel it in his hands. Nana's fingers are knobbly, her veins prominent, but Clement's hands feel like Mordecai's and Daddy's, anywhere from adolescent to middle-aged. He has high cheekbones, long eyelashes, and soft, full lips, thick hair that brushes his shoulders. I was locked in Zilpah's bedroom when Hagar brought him home, so I don't know what he normally smells like. I imagine something more pleasant than fear and blood. I sniff him again, behind his ear, then at the base of his neck, but it's been a week, whatever cologne or body wash he had before is long gone.

When I start to pull away, Clement follows me, as much as he can, sort of presses his face into the crook of my neck before I step back entirely. I pat his head, and he leans into the touch, more desperate and docile than any of the previous men. Cal let me hug him, but he couldn't have been more than four or five years old, he hadn't learned to act tough yet. I can't imagine that Daddy, who hates weak men almost as much as he hates disobedient women, has been going easy on poor Clement. He's still intact so far, no severe injuries, although I imagine kneeling on concrete for a week straight is agonizing all on its own.

I wish I could tell him I'd set him free if I could; the most I can do is remember his name. Hagar knows all their names, but Daddy never asks for them, and she never tells anyone else. To her, they're sinners to be punished, a collection of parts to be harvested, eaten, and repurposed. I remember their names at every meal, every time I touch Hagar's leather furniture, and I know she remembers their names, too; she keeps everything she possibly can, vials of blood and organs preserved in ethanol, skulls on her shelves, and I've felt the jars, leather labels in front of cool glass jars. All their names- their real names- are carved there, surrounded by what I think are floral designs. Hagar always, always smells like blood, but I'm the only one who notices.

Zilpah

Zilthai never spends the night in the room we're supposed to share. I think she sleeps in different places, the attic and the basement in winter, maybe the barn loft in summer. She's here now, though, crawling around on the floor, so fast it looks unnatural. She started crawling again after Daddy had to take her eyes out, slowly at first, then faster and faster. She *can* walk, and she sometimes does, but I can tell she likes crawling better. Not so far to fall, I think, and she can feel more, "see" her surroundings better.

Zilthai freezes and whips her head towards me the second the door opens- I wonder if she can feel the air change, somehow, or if stepping on the floorboards makes them move enough for her to sense it, but either way her nostrils flare for a moment before she relaxes, jumps to her feet and walks to my side, grabs my hand to kiss the back of it with a clumsy bow. Sometimes she bites me, sometimes she kisses me, sometimes she ignores me all together.

"Ladies curtsy," I say uselessly. Nana used to give us etiquette lessons in the living room, but Zilthai never cared about them, definitely won't be using them now. Daddy stopped trying to get her under control when she bit the skin off his fingertip- it was awful, the way she latched on and jerked back so fast it all came off like a glove. Daddy told us it's actually called a "degloving injury". I don't know what he told the doctors when Mordecai drove him into town. There are crazy people in the outside world, I've seen them in movies, violent lunatics who attack each other over nothing, filthy drug addicts living in the street, so maybe they just assumed it was one of those sinners.

Zilthai drops my hand and falls to the ground again, goes back to whatever she was doing before. I sit on the edge of my bed, and she finally stops when her hand grazes a bracelet I left on the floor, snatches it up and rubs it between her palms, licks it, then just sits still. Hagar made it for me a long time ago as a birthday present, tried to give one to Zilthai but she threw hers away or hid it somewhere, I don't know which. That was when Mordecai brought the twins home, identical twins I met briefly before Daddy took them to the barn, and Hagar spent more than a week crafting the bracelets for us. She braided their hair into thin rope, strung it with their teeth, and carved our names into small strips of their leather. I liked the bracelets, but Zilthai never wore hers.

While she turns the bracelet slowly in her hands, I lay on my side and think of the sinners in our barn. I did a bad job taking care of them today, but it isn't my fault; the girl cursed me, tried to get away from me, and the man was crying so much I couldn't stand him. He doesn't cry like a damned sinner or a monster or an animal, he cries like Hagar and Nana. He cries like me. I'll do better tomorrow, but I couldn't handle it today, seeing him cry like that. The girl is easy, the girl swears and screams and tries to bite; if the man was feral like her, I could hose him down and feed him without any problems. He acts almost like a person, and I wish he'd stop pretending, he's making me feel sick and sad, making my stomach churn at the thought of eating him.

Zilthai

I trace Zilpah's name over and over and over again, always lingering on the little cross Hagar put after it. She made these before I lost my eyes, but I don't quite remember what they looked like. I remember the crosses, though, remember feeling sick when I unwrapped the little package. She put them in tiny pink boxes, on a bed of expensive tissue paper Daddy bought her, and she beamed when we opened them, clapped her hands together and said something to Zilpah. There was a note under my bracelet. *For my precious little sister, with love from Hagar.* She looked so genuine, so happy, and I noticed her frowning when I wouldn't wear mine.

We used to have more of a relationship- used to have a better relationship than I had with Zilpah, because Daddy says sign language is the devil's work and Zilpah is only semi-literate. Hagar taught me to read with Daddy's blessing, and for years that was how we communicated, until he cut my eyes out. Now, she traces letters on my palm when she *has* to talk to me. She never *wants* to talk to me anymore.

I feel the floorboards shift when Zilpah gets out of bed too heavily, too fast, and snarl at her before she can get close to me. I'd looked for the bracelet in her jewelry box, first, an antique originally owned by Nana's grandmother, but Zilpah is always leaving things scattered around randomly. While she can cook if Hagar stands over her shoulder and tells her exactly what to do, cleaning is beyond her. She forgets where everything goes, tosses jewelry and clothes aside without thinking, and I want to bite her for being so careless with the last remnants of a human life. The twins had names, Sarah and Margaret, they were real people with names and souls, and I don't even know which twin Hagar used for which bracelet, whether it was Sarah or Margaret my sister threw to the floor so casually.

I haven't slept in our room in ages. Our mother designed it for us before we were even born, soft pastel pink with doves painted on the walls. Hagar says our mother understood our souls when we were still inside her, as soon as she knew she was pregnant, and she knew she was pregnant long before she started showing. She always knew, like a witch. She knew we'd be girls, knew we'd be twins, predicted she'd die delivering us, but that wasn't true. She drowned herself in the river a mile away as soon as she could walk again, so Hagar nursed us with goat's milk. She claims she mixed drops of her own blood into it.

It's still August, too hot to be inside anyway- I don't know how the rest of them stand it- so I slip back outside, down the well-worn path to the barn. I could make it out with just my feet, but I like crawling, I'm faster on all fours than on two legs and I think it puts Daddy and Mordecai off, too. Our mother was Daddy's little sister, and I'm sixteen now, the same age as her when she had Mordecai. Daddy was thirty, he'd just moved his family "off grid" to start a new, pure, holy life; when Mordecai was born completely normal, he took it as a sign from God that his mission was righteous. When Hagar was born with mild deformities, he said it was a coincidence, and by the time he realized I was deaf and Zilpah was retarded, our mother was already gone. Nana told me we'd all be normal if we weren't inbred, back when she could still write.

No one comes up to the barn loft except me; I don't think anyone else even knows about my little nest of blankets and pillows. Daddy divided the barn into two sections, the pens and the slaughterhouse, and he doesn't care what I do as long as I stay out of the latter. It reeks up here, especially in the heat of summer, but it's better than staying in his house, where Mordecai thinks he's in love with me.

Zilpah

"You're bleeding."

"Go fuck yourself," Harlot responds at once, spitting at me. She's bleeding down her legs, but it's too early for Daddy to have punished her yet, he won't be here for a few more hours.

"You're dirty."

"Yeah? God, I wonder how that happened!"

"'Thou shalt not take the name of the Lord thy God in vain', Harlot."

"What are you, a pilgrim? Harlot? Fuck's that even mean?"

"Whore. Prostitute."

"Oh, get fucked," she snaps. Her canine teeth are sharper than a person's, I think, sharp like a snake's.

"You're bleeding."

"I'll cut your goddamn throat and-"

"'Thou shalt not take the name of the Lord thy God in vain.'"

"Goddamn," she shrieks. In the next pen over, Sodomite cries out, probably scared by the sudden high-pitched noise.

"'Thou shalt not take the name of the Lord thy God in vain'. You scared him. The man."

"And fuck you too, pussy," Harlot screams, at Sodomite, I guess, but she can't turn her head with the chains tight around her neck. "Goddamn, crybaby fuckin' bitch, can't fuckin' sleep with that little shitstain cryin' all goddamn night in this-"

"'Thou shalt not take the name of the Lord thy God in vain.'"

"Get a little closer, cunt, I'll send you to meet your fuckin' God, see what the hell He says to you!"

"God loves me. God loves my family."

"*Jesus loves me, this I know, for the Bible tells me so,*" Harlot sings, in an awful, mocking tone. "Who told you God loves you, huh? Your daddy? 'Cause the Bible don't say jackshit 'bout *this*, you psycho freak."

"Yes, Daddy told us."

"*Jesus loves me, this I know,*" Harlot repeats. She has a voice like nails on a chalkboard. "*Jesus loves me, He who died, Heaven's gate to open wide-*"

I spray her in the face with the hose to make her shut up, but she just spits the water out and keeps singing once I move it lower, trying to clean her up as best I can while keeping my distance. "You're a bad singer. Your voice is so ugly."

"*He will wash away my sin, let His little child come in,*" Harlot answers, louder now that she knows she's bothering me, "*Jesus loves me, this I know, as He loved so long ago.* You believe in Jesus, huh? You ever read the New Testament?"

"No."

"Has your daddy?"

"Probably."

"But he ain't read it to you?"

"He says Jesus was too nice. Daddy says God hates sinners. Sinners burn in Hell."

"What the fuck kinda Christians are y'all, anyway? Ain't Christ s'posed to be important?"

"Daddy used to be a Southern Baptist preacher."

"Oh, well, that checks out."

"You're still bleeding."

"I'm on my period, retard."

"You're filthy. You're a filthy whore," I say, raising my voice more than I have before, and Harlot grins wickedly.

"You mad, *retard*? What, you don't like that, huh? You don't like bein' a fuckin' retarded cunt?"

"You'll burn in Hell!" I scream, kicking the water I was supposed to give her over. "You'll burn in Hell forever! Forever and ever and ever, because God hates you!"

"Yeah, whatever, goddamn retard bitch," Harlot yells after me when I turn to walk out, slamming the gate too hard and failing to lock it twice before my hands stop shaking. I can still hear her singing as I unlock Sodomite's gate, "*Jesus loves me, this I know, for the Bible tells me so...*"

Sodomite flinches as soon as I walk in, and I can see that Daddy's hurt him more than Harlot, either because he's been here longer or because he deserves it more. He has a black eye, his ribs are bruised, and there are nails driven into his thighs, blood crusted over his split lips. "You smell bad," I snap at him, then close my eyes and try to steady myself. It's not his fault Harlot is an evil whore, a monster, I shouldn't be mad at him- but he's evil, too, he's a sinner. I should always be mad at them, the same way Hagar is.

"I have- I have a daughter," Sodomite whimpers, his voice thick, "I have a d- a- a daughter who's... your age, please. You- y-you remind me of- of her, please, you don't have to... to do this..."

"Is she a sinner, too?"

"I'm not- I- I d-don't un-un-understand-"

"Be quiet. Stop crying!"

"Please- pl- please, I didn't- I- I haven't done an-anything-"

"You're a sinner. You're a filthy sinner."

"Please, please, please," Sodomite wails, and for a second I think he's struggling against the chains, but he's just rocking back and forth, sobbing. In the other pen, Harlot keeps singing, *Jesus loves me, this I know,* and I hate them both, they're both horrible, her for being so cruel and him for crying like this, trying to make me feel guilty when he isn't even human, he's just a damned sinner, his daughter is evil, too, she should be here with him now.

"SHUT UP!" I scream, turning the hose on to make him stop, but he just gags and tries to get away, he's still crying, so I try to close my eyes and ears like Zilthai, wash him off as best I can and take the food with me when I leave. He can't eat like that, anyway, he's crying too hard. He'd just choke to death, and then Daddy wouldn't be able to punish him like he deserves.

Hagar is in the garden when I run outside, and she stands up to greet me, her smile fading when she sees how close I am to tears. "What's wrong?"

"I hate them! She's evil- Harlot- the girl, she called me retarded, she took the Lord's name in vain, and the man won't stop crying."

"Oh," Hagar says, glancing back at the barn. "Oh, darling, I'm sorry. They're all like that. Sinners are all the same, nasty mongrels living in filth, living like pigs. You'll get used to it soon. Perseverance is the key, do you understand? Soon, you'll be able to ignore them completely. Dogs cry, too, you know- they whimper and whine, but they're not human. You mustn't be upset by his... theatrics. And don't listen to anything that whore tells you." She pats my cheek, smiling softly, the sun lighting her golden hair from behind like a halo. "I have complete faith in you, my precious one. Don't be fooled by anything they say to you, and always remember that they deserve every minute of it."

Zilthai

Clement's fingernails have been torn out. I sit next to him, hold my palm out for him, and can't help grimacing at the raw, wet sensation of unprotected nailbeds. *H-E-L-P M-E.* I shake my head, *no,* trace *S-T-O-P* on his chest. *Stop asking, stop crying, stop hoping I'll save you.* Zilpah did a better job of cleaning him today, at least, but his chapped lips and the stronger stench of ammonia tells me hasn't been drinking enough water, if any. I pat his shoulder and crawl to the metal bowl Zilpah is supposed to give them water in. I understand why she hasn't- she has to hold it to their mouths, force them to lap at it like dogs, and she doesn't want to be close to them, I can tell. I fumble with the bowl and the hose for a minute before bringing it back over to Clement.

I keep a hand on his head while he drinks, stroking his hair. He gulps down the entire bowl in seconds, then leans into my hand ever so slightly, as much as he can chained up like this. I'm scared he'll throw up if I give him more water, so I just let him nuzzle at my hand, hesitate for a second before tracing *S-O-R-R-Y* on his chest. He doesn't react. After a few minutes, I lean forward, kiss his cheek, and stand to leave, to check on the girl again.

She won't let me close enough to trace a message, throws her head like a horse and tries to bite me when I bring her water, and I finally give up after an hour, scurry dejectedly back up to my loft. The girl, I know, will never let me help her, and Clement still seems to think I can save him. I don't want to give him false hope, but I can't help visiting him, offering any small comfort I can. He's so sweet to me, more than anyone before him- they all hated me, I could feel it in their tensed muscles, but as far as I can tell, Clement genuinely relaxes around me, thinks I'm an ally or a friend. *You're going to die here,* I want to tell him, *and no one else will ever know. I'm the only one who'll care, and I'll still eat you. Don't think I'm your friend, Clement. I'm nobody's knight in shining armor.*

Zilpah

Zilthai sleeps in the barn, and I know she doesn't want me following her, but I have to wonder what she gets out of it. Isn't it nicer inside? We've never been able to talk much- before she was blind, Hagar wrote down what I wanted to say to her, because I've never been great at writing. I don't know how to get through to her now, no one does. Hagar says she lost her mind when Daddy tore her eyes out. I hate thinking about it, I remember how she screamed- like it was yesterday- I'd never heard her scream before. I didn't know deaf people could scream.

I'm not sure if she'll notice me following her. Probably not, as long as I'm careful where I step; it reeks in the barn, she can't possibly smell me over the awful stench we can't wash away. I only wanted to see where she sleeps, but now I'm watching her give Sodomite water, petting his head like he's some kind of puppy. I should tell Daddy what she's doing, but then he'll know I haven't been doing my job all the way. I watch Zilthai hold her hand behind the man's back, react to something- he must be tracing letters on her palm. He starts crying as soon as she leaves, and even though he must know she's deaf by now, he calls out after her, "Come back, please, please, don't-don't leave- please..."

"Can you shut the fuck up?" Harlot barks from her pen, and Sodomite whimpers, bites his lip. Neither of them can see me from here.

"I'm s- I'm sorry," he manages.

"Does she talk?" Harlot asks after a second. Her voice is hoarse from so much cursing, screaming, making it worse for herself.

"Who?"

"The crazy girl, dipshit. The blind one."

"She- um- she's deaf, I think."

"Blind and deaf?"

"Th-th-think so. Yeah."

"And what's wrong with *you*?"

"Nothing's wrong with- there's nothing wrong with me," Sodomite says, sounding a tiny bit offended.

"N-n-n-nothing's wr-wr-wrong with m-m-me," Harlot mocks in a high-pitched voice. "The hell there ain't, fucking freak."

"I'm... I'm only... scared," Sodomite says softly.

"Pussy," Harlot says. "No wonder nobody fuckin' likes you."

"Your f- fa- your family must, must, um, must be looking for y-y-for you?"

"Shut the fuck up, Clement." She falls quiet for a second, then asks, "D'you really have a daughter? You said y'ain't got no fam'ly, before."

"Oh. No, I... I don't. I just th-I thought- maybe-"

"What, she'll let you go if you got a fam'ly?"

"I don't- I don't know. I guess." He sounds like he's about to cry again.

"Dumbass. You're gonna die here. You know you're gonna die here, right?"

"No," the man whimpers.

"Yes, you are. We're gonna fucking *die here!*" Harlot's voice raises into a shrill scream, and Sodomite bursts into tears. A board creaks up in the loft, and I decide it's time to leave. Zilthai is deaf, I remind myself, there's a reason she can handle sleeping above them, she can't hear how miserable the girl sounded. I don't want to hear that kind of awful screaming again, the fear and pain and fury in Harlot's voice, don't want to think about how nearly human she sounded.

Instead of focusing on Harlot's voice, I think about the man, Sodomite, how he lied to me. I shouldn't be surprised- they're sinners, of course he's a liar, too, but I can't understand why he'd tell me that particular lie. Why would I care if he has a daughter, especially one my age? Why does he *think* I care? If he just cursed at me and screamed and carried on, like Harlot, I wouldn't give it any thought, but he acts like I'm a person, like he can reason with me. And I *am* a person, of course, but *he* isn't. Hagar told me they get confused, the sinners, they think *we're* the monsters. I'm so distracted that I bump into Mordecai walking through the living room, and he lights up, grabs my arm and drags me onto Hagar's leather couch. She's such a brilliant artist, but right now I can't help thinking of Clement's freckled skin and I feel a little sick.

"What's on your mind, honey?" Mordecai asks, resting a comforting hand on my thigh.

"The man lied to me today."

"Oh? What about?"

"He said he has a daughter my age."

"Well, he's a little young to have a teenage daughter, but maybe if he-"

"I heard him say he lied. He told the girl."

"In front of you?"

"I was hiding. Watching Zilthai."

"What was she doing out there?"

"Uh..." I blush, look at my lap. "I couldn't feed them. They make me... sad. She gave him water."

"They deserve it, honey. Don't fall for whatever nonsense they try to tell you."

"Why did he lie?"

"He wants you to feel sorry for him."

"But why does he think I care about his daughter?"

"Who knows?" Mordecai shrugs, stretches. "I'm going to bed, Zilpah. Get some rest."

"His daughter wouldn't be like me," I say, but he's already leaving, he doesn't hear me. Finally, it hits me- the man thought I could relate to a girl my age, a girl from the outside world, a sinful, evil girl, but a girl he thinks would be normal. He thinks I'm someone like him, and I don't know how that makes me feel, but I don't like it.

Zilthai

Clement is getting more and more attached to me, and I wish I could stay away from him, I've never liked one of the sinners so much. He asks for comfort instead of salvation now, his trembling, bloody fingers tracing *H-O-L-D M-E*, and I do what he wants, I wrap my arms around him and let him hide his face in my neck, snuggling up to me like a puppy. The girl still won't have anything to do with me, won't accept food or water, and I like her, too, I can't help but admire her stubborn strength. I have no idea if Zilpah's successfully getting her to drink or if she intends to kill herself via dehydration; if it's the latter, I want to tell her she's making the right choice, otherwise she'll be here for months on end before Daddy takes her to the slaughterhouse.

F-A-M-I-L-Y, I trace onto Clement's palm, tap his chest and cock my head to the side, hoping to convey the question clearly, *do you have a family?* He has to be half-insane by now, exhausted, starving, thirsty, miserable beyond what I can imagine- I'm afraid he'd lose track of the letters if I attempted a longer sentence. After a few tries, he responds, *N-O.*

F-R-I-E-N-D-S

N-O

A-N-Y-O-N-E

Y-O-U

I pull my hand back, stroke his hair and sigh. If I could really talk to him, I'd ask him who he is, why there's no one waiting on him, why the kindness of a feral girl in a hellish torture chamber means so much to him, but I have no way to ask him much more than I already have. Clement nuzzles against my palm, and again I'm reminded of a dog, I imagine somehow stealing the key and setting him loose- but where would he go? A hundred miles deep in the Texas wilderness, seriously injured, probably getting sick, how far could he possibly get before Daddy and Mordecai track him down? If I was a better person, I'd strangle him right now, before the worst of it starts, before he becomes unrecognizable to himself, but I've never been good. Clement is the closest thing I've ever had to a pet, and I want one pure thing in my life, one living thing that really, truly loves me, one thing to make me feel human.

Zilpah

"Why do they have to stay alive so long?" I ask Hagar, pulling up weeds in the garden.

"They must be punished," she replies calmly.

"But they'll go to Hell when they die. Why does Daddy have to torture them here?"

"It's not our place to question God's will."

"How does Daddy know God's will?"

"What's got into you today?" Hagar stops working, turns to frown at me. "You know, Zilthai started asking those questions right before she tried to run away. Don't you remember?"

"I think so?"

"Daddy is carrying out God's will here on Earth," Hagar says firmly. I hear someone scream from the barn, but I can't tell if it's the man or the girl.

"You know their names," I say cautiously.

"So do you," she points out. They always have supper with us, that first night- Mordecai brings them home, invites them to eat with us, Hagar slips something into their food, and they wake up in the barn. Up until very recently, that was all I saw of them until it was time to process the meat.

"You remember them, though." It's not safe to eat their brains, Daddy says, so Hagar keeps them preserved in ethanol, labels every jar with their real names carved into a strip of leather.

"I suppose I do."

"Why do you label the jars with their names?"

"Because so many of them have committed the same sin. I couldn't very well have four jars labeled 'adulteress'."

"Oh." I pull up another weed. "The man's name is Clement."

"Yes, I know. The girl is Ebba."

"Emma?"

"No, Ebba. She made that very clear." I hadn't been paying attention to her when we had supper. Mordecai brought her home drunk, said he picked her up at a bar, a den of iniquity.

"I've never heard that."

"Well, she's probably never heard any of our names, either. They don't read the Bible out there."

"I think she's Christian."

"She's a heathen."

"She keeps singing this song about Jesus. '*Jesus loves me, this I know, for the Bible tells me so*'."

"I hope you're not listening to anything they tell you, Zilpah?"

"Not really."

"They're all damned sinners and nothing more. Don't let them lead you astray with their silver tongues."

"I won't. I promise."

When I bring them food, Ebba- the girl, I tell myself, nothing but the girl, but I can't help calling her by name- is missing her teeth. All her teeth. She runs her tongue over her still-bleeding gums and spits at me when I walk up to her. "Not hungry," she says thickly.

"Your name is Ebba."

"Yeah? And what about it?"

"What does it mean?"

"Strength of a boar," she says after a long pause. "How long before y'all kill me?"

"Daddy kills the sinners. Not me."

"How long?"

"I don't know. Usually a few months. Maybe a year, at the longest."

"A year," Ebba repeats emotionlessly.

"That only happened once. It won't be that long."

"I can't eat that," she points out, nodding slightly at the food I've brought, all of which does, I guess, have to be chewed.

"That's too bad. Do you want water?"

"Up yours."

"What?"

"Y'know, I thought your daddy was gonna cut my junk up, like FGM.

Heard what he did to that poor bastard next door." She tilts her head in Clement's direction, as much as she can. "Hasn't touched it yet, though. Just ripped all my damn teeth out. Not too bad, I guess, I can always get dentures, huh?"

"You will not leave this place alive."

"I used to dream 'bout biting your throat out, cunt. You know that? I could find another way, now. Bash your fuckin' skull in."

"Do you want water?"

"Go fuck yourself."

I leave her alone, walk into Clement's pen, and flinch back when I see what Daddy did to him. I'd never seen a naked man before I started bring him food and water, and I have to admit I stared at him for a few seconds the first time, almost wanted to touch between his legs out of curiosity, but now he looks more like me. There's an ugly, jaggedly stitched-up red wound where his private parts were. At least he still has all his teeth, as far as I can tell. "Does that hurt?" I ask. Ebba laughs from the next pen over, mutters something that sounds a lot like *idiot*.

Clement nods once, avoiding my gaze. "How- how- h-how- are, um, a-a-are... y-you?" he manages. He's shaking, deathly pale, and his lips are turning blue.

"Are you cold?"

"Wanna go home," Clement says, eyes empty. "C-can- can I- can I, can I go home?"

"No."

"I w- I w- I want, I wanna go home."

"Eat," I tell him, holding the bread Hagar made to his lips. He obeys me like an automaton, and I notice a trickle of urine wetting his thighs, flinch back in disgust. I guess he can't control it anymore, not without his... thing. I don't know what it's called.

"Please, please, let- let m-me go," he whispers.

"Drink." He drinks the water just as mechanically. "Zilthai likes you."

"Oh. She- she's- she's my... fr- friend."

"She's going to eat you. Daddy's going to kill you, and we're all going to eat you."

"She... she's my, um, my friend."

"She's his only friend," Ebba calls from the other pen, laughing high and mean. "Nobody else can stand the little bitch. Nobody's waiting for him."

"Do you have a family?" I ask Clement, and he shakes his head slowly, no.

"I... I asked... I asked a w- a w- a woman, um, um, to m-mar-marry me," he whispers. "She... she said, sh- she said-"

"I said *no*," Ebba yells. "Goddamn creep."

Zilthai

I once walked in on Hagar pulling her own teeth out with pliers, before I lost my eyes. It looked like she was screaming, but she kept doing it for weeks, pulling her teeth one at a time until she ran out. I never saw them in jewelry, so I don't know what she did with them, and I never asked her why she did it. She's a little bit fixated on teeth, I think- she uses everything she can for art, but the teeth are her favorites, she's always wearing someone's teeth. Bracelets, anklets, necklaces, earrings, hair clips, and rings, I've never seen Hagar without a flash of dull yellow-white somewhere on her body, easy enough to miss or write off as fakes, some kind of bizarre fashion statement. She was wearing a heavy cross necklace the day Daddy cut my eyes out, a cross made of children's teeth wired together and strung on a rope of silky hair. She didn't smile or frown, didn't look away like Zilpah and Mordecai did, just watched in total silence.

Daddy hasn't hurt me since then. He's tried to pet my head, but I always snap at him and crawl away, I won't let him near me. I never realized he cared about my relationships with the sinners until tonight, when I find Clement's fingers docked at the knuckle, his newly empty eye sockets stuffed with cotton, his tongue cut out. He doesn't move at all when I scream right next to his ear, just noses at my neck, blind and deaf and mute as me, unable to communicate in any way at all without fingers to trace letters, and I'd bet a million dollars Daddy did it to spite me, saw how much I like him and locked him away from me, guaranteed he'll never speak to me again.

Zilpah

I find Zilthai asleep next to Clement in the morning, and when I step close to him she tries to bite me. I feel a little sick, looking at him- I don't know if this is what Daddy always does to the sinners, but Clement looks like something out of a nightmare. He was pretty when he got here, Nana sighed that he was an adorable young man, it was too bad, and now he makes me want to throw up. It might be my fault; I told Daddy that Zilthai is obsessed with him. He keeps trying to move his head, fresh blood occasionally trickling from his ears, and making these awful, inhuman little noises.

"I have to feed him," I yell at Zilthai, who snarls, moves in front of him like he's her pet. I suppose he is. Finally, I grab her arm, trace *F-U-D* (I think that spells "food" but I've been wrong before), and Zilthai hesitates, then seems to understand and pulls back, crouches a foot away while I try to feed Clement. He can't quite get the hang of it without his tongue, and by the time I'm done there's more food down his front than in his mouth. I help him drink some water, then hose him off and leave him with my sister, who, if she knows what's good for her, will leave before Daddy shows up.

"What'd he do to him?" Ebba asks when I walk into her pen, licking her lips.

"You're getting a rash," I tell her. "Around your mouth. It looks bad. You look ugly."

"Yeah, well, you ain't no prize yourself, cunt," Ebba says, sounding bored. "What'd your daddy do to Clement? He ain't tried to talk to me since yesterday, and he didn't answer when I yelled at him."

"He made him like Zilthai," I say softly.

"What, the deafblind girl? How?" She looks disgusted, and I shuffle my feet awkwardly.

"He cut his eyes out. He did something to his ears, too, but I don't know what. And his tongue and fingers are gone."

"Fuck," Ebba breathes. "God, you people are so fucked."

"'Thou shalt not'-"

"Don't you *dare* preach at me after what y'all done to that man," Ebba says sharply, and I hesitate, unsure how to respond.

"He's a sinner," I mutter to the ground.

"Hell, he's just a... he's creepy, but he didn't deserve that. Not like he was a rapist or nothin'. He wadn't half as bad as you."

"He asked you to marry him? Here?"

"No," Ebba says, licking her lips again. "No, we... nah. I'm a waitress." She pauses. "I *was* a waitress. I don't think Clement had any friends or fam'ly or nobody', and he came to my diner a lot, didn't talk much. I thought he was sweet, I guess. Shy. Kinda cute, but he's... shit, maybe a decade older'n me? I'm eighteen, y'know. I'm only eighteen." She watches my face for a reaction, then sighs and continues, "He really didn't talk to me much till he asked me to marry him. I was goin' home after work, 'bout nine, and he followed me outside, said he was in love with me, he was so lonely, begged me to marry him. He gave me a ring." She wrinkles her nose up in disgust. "I barely knew him."

"You said no?"

"I slapped him and told him to go kill hisself if he's so fuckin' lonely."

"Oh."

"Didn't think he'd do it. Didn't want him to end up here," Ebba mutters.

"You met Mordecai at a bar," I say slowly, and she nods. "Did you tell him about Clement proposing?"

"Might of done. I was fucked up."

"You're both sinners."

"They ever tell you why? What sin did I commit, huh? What the hell we done that's worse than all this shit?"

"You... you're a whore, and he's a sodomite."

"Shit, bitch, I don't even know what 'sodomite' means, but I ain't no whore."

"'Sodomite' means..." I bite my lip. "I'll ask Hagar."

"Go to Hell," Ebba mutters, closing her eyes, "you can all go straight to Hell."

Zilthai

For the first time since she's been here, the girl lets me touch her. I spent longer than usual with Clement, stroking his hair and fussing over him, but I still go to the girl, and I jump back in spite of myself when she doesn't fight me. I hold my palm so she can write on it, and after a minute, she finally tells me her name. I've never heard of anyone named Ebba before; I think it's beautiful.

H-E-L-P U-S, she writes after a moment, and I turn my head toward Clement's pen even though I can't see it, I can't stop myself. I like him, he's docile and sweet and gentle, and Daddy had no right, no right at all, to hurt him like that, lock him away in his body for whatever remains of his life.

I take a deep breath, gather my courage, and write, *H-O-W*.

BLUE MOON

By Jacklyn Baker

THE MOON HAD COME A second time this month. It was large in the sky, bright and full. But it was silver in color, not blue. Adriana had never understood why they called it a "blue moon."

She stared at it while waiting for the 6:58 bus to arrive. It was past 9:00 now—the bus had broken down and according to the announcement online the other buses that had already finished their daily circuits were working to complete Route 4 now.

When the bus finally did come, it would pick her up from Speight Avenue and take her six stops to 11th Street to her tiny apartment on the ground floor of a thirty year-old building that needed a paint job and a new HVAC system. She would unlock her door and shuffle her heavy bag off her shoulder without taking more than two steps into the living room. She would change into comfy pants, take off her bra, and heat up some form of microwavable dinner. Then she would sit on the couch and study her Organic Chemistry book until she couldn't see straight anymore. Then she would wake up at 5:30 a.m., go to her shift at the coffee shop, then her classes, then her shift at the library. And then she'd wait for the 6:58 and do it all over again.

It was just bad luck that it hadn't happened that way today.

A bus finally rolled to a stop in front of her, creaking on its axels and hissing at her as if to warn her away from it. It certainly felt like some beast come to swallow her whole.

Adriana stared at the moon until the vehicle's doors opened. A fleeting thought about running away with the man in the moon crossed her mind and then she dismissed it for the flight of fancy it was.

The thing about running away with any man was the inevitable consequences that came with it. Adriana woke six days after the night of the blue moon, threw up into her bedside trash can, and immediately knew she was pregnant. She couldn't explain how she knew—some strange sense that she was no longer alone maybe—but she knew. A trip to the Student Life Center clinic at the cost of a missed Anatomy class confirmed this. She was two weeks into an unexpected pregnancy.

She didn't know what to do.

More importantly, she didn't know how it was possible in the first place.

She hadn't had sex in the two months since the semester started. She didn't have the time for it.

When the doctor kindly tried to discuss her options, Adriana dismissed her. She rose from the examination table, paper sheet crinkling loudly, picked up her purse, and walked out of the room.

Adriana wrestled with her dilemma alone, sat on the lumpy couch in her apartment. She loathed to tell her mother. Although the woman was only thirty minutes outside of Waco, she would offer no comfort and certainly no assistance. Her classmates and coworkers were friendly, but not friends. Adriana knew she couldn't keep the baby, but she also knew she couldn't go through with the act of getting rid of it. She'd have to give it away. There was really no other choice.

She waited until after midterms—she owed herself that much at least after all her hard work—and then she went to a doctor off-campus. This one was a proper OB/GYN. She picked a man in his late forties called Dr. Moorjani, who officed in the Women's and Children's Center of the Hillcrest Hospital for no other reason than that he had a time slot available during her

Anatomy class, which was quickly becoming the go-to class to skip for doctor's appointments.

Adriana waited an unreasonable amount of time for the doctor to finally see her, sitting in the sterile, beige room and staring at a diagram of a uterus for nearly an hour after her appointment was due to start. Too bad that wasn't the section they were covering in Anatomy right now.

When Dr. Moorjani finally concluded the examination, the results were the same, except that this doctor told her she was closer to two months into her pregnancy rather than, according to the initial doctor, what would be just over four weeks now. That made more sense. The S.L.C. doctors just weren't equipped to properly evaluate a pregnancy, that was all. This pregnancy must be from before school started and she'd had some spotting that she thought was her period last month. She questioned the doctor about it, but he told her everything was normal and a little bleeding early-on isn't unheard of. The baby was fine.

When Dr. Moorjani asked if she knew who the father might be, Adriana had to admit that she didn't. Her last sexual encounter had been a one-night stand. She hadn't gotten a number or even a last name.

"Baby Lawrence then," Dr. Moorjani said with an easy acceptance, making a note in mother and baby's file.

But it didn't sit right with Adriana when she knew she wouldn't be keeping it.

Three weeks later, Adriana was showing. Her belly had swollen overnight. She stood in the full-length mirror on the back of her bedroom door for fifteen minutes, turned sideways and staring at the…growth. It was beginning to feel less like a baby was in there and more like a parasite, like her belly would just swell and swell until it burst like a balloon and whatever was inside crawled out and left her hollow and bloodless.

Adriana's breath stuttered. She stopped that train of thought right there. That was ridiculous. The possibility of a more realistic complication, however, was not ridiculous. She forced herself away from the mirror.

Throughout the morning her coworkers offered their congratulations, asking her why she hadn't told them. The answer was simple. She'd thought she had more time to do it.

The minute his office opened, Adriana called and moved her next visit with Dr. Moorjani up to his earliest available time. He saw her that afternoon (Anatomy class again).

The doctor's brow furrowed to see her belly and arranged for an ultrasound immediately.

He spread the cold gel over her stomach, creating involuntary spasms in Adriana's muscles, then moved the wand around until he found what he was looking for.

Then he turned the machine off and sat there silently.

"Dr. Moorjani?" Adriana said with a hint of alarm. This morning's vision of her stomach bursting apart came back in a flash of remembrance.

He shook his head. "I'm sorry, Miss Lawrence. The baby looks perfectly fine, but…let me just look at your file again."

He did and he came away from it confused.

"It's a boy," he told her, but he still looked completely flummoxed.

"Okay. And?"

"And I shouldn't be able to determine the sex yet. It should be another two weeks before we can tell, but…well, you look to be about sixteen weeks along now."

Adriana jolted, her elbow knocking into the ultrasound machine. "Sixteen—! How can that be? I was only nine weeks along three weeks ago."

The man looked down at the papers again and flipped one over. "Perhaps I was mistaken."

Adriana couldn't help the flare of anger. "Mistaken? Do you think you could maybe not be mistaken please?"

The doctor blinked, then lowered the file to give her his full attention. "Yes. Yes, of course, I apologize, Miss Lawrence. I didn't mean to upset you. Let me make some phone calls.

Come back the same time next week?"

Why not? Adriana thought. I'm already failing Anatomy anyway.

When it first kicked, Adriana dropped a cup of coffee. It was such a strong kick, it startled her as much as the ceiling falling down might have. The loud clatter of the paper cup and the slosh of liquid against tile drew the attention of patrons and employees alike. The steaming coffee was all over the floor. Some of it had splashed up and was scalding the skin beneath

Adriana's pant leg.

"Adriana?" came the concerned voice of her shift manager, Elizabeth. "Are you all right?"

"I—" Adriana swallowed, her sentence cut short by another rattling kick. "Yeah. Yeah, fine."

Elizabeth frowned, unconvinced. "Why don't you sit down for a few minutes? I'll remake that drink. Okay?"

When Elizabeth put her hand on her arm, Adriana noticed the steadiness of her touch against her own shaking limbs. Sitting might not be so bad an idea after all. She nodded. "Okay."

Adriana caught the eye of the customer whose drink she had dropped as Elizabeth ushered her out of the workspace. He was giving her a look like there was something wrong with her.

Maybe there was.

At their follow-up appointment Dr. Moorjani had called in a second doctor to consult on her visit.

"It's not that we think that there's anything to worry about, but I'd like a second opinion," Dr. Moorjani explained. "So we can be absolutely certain nothing's wrong. No mistakes. Is it alright if Dr. Dillihunt examines you as well?"

Dr. Dillihunt, a woman with graying blonde hair, smiled pleasantly at her. Adriana didn't like the sound of "second opinion," but gave her permission.

The conclusion was not good.

The baby had reached what her doctor and the consulting doctor both deemed to be eighteen weeks.

"It's only been one week!" Adriana exclaimed. "How could it be two weeks further along?"

Her OB/GYN shook his head. "I don't know. We'll want to run some tests..." he prodded gently.

Dr. Dillihunt was rapidly flipping back and forth between the pages in her file, a look like fascination on her face.

Adriana pressed her palms into her eyes. "Fine. Do what you have to."

By the following week Adriana was twenty weeks along according to both Dr. Moorjani and Dr. Dillihunt.

A whole team of doctors was brought in to poke and prod at her, but not one held any more answers for the unusual growth rate than the last. Adriana spent more time in a doctor's office than she did in a classroom. They ran blood panels and performed scans and went over her family's medical history with a fine-tooth comb. They picked apart her diet and shined a light in her eye more times than she thought was strictly necessary. They monitored her for seventy-two hours straight and recorded every move she made.

The school marked all of her courses as Incompletes. It was for the best. She was going to have to reconsider her field of study anyway. Working in research held a lot less appeal now after being given the guinea pig treatment and listening to doctors talk about the medical journals they would write about her.

Her belly continued to swell. It protruded past her breasts now. Her back was beginning to ache. Her clothes were getting tighter.

She took down the mirror in her bedroom.

Three weeks later and all the medical experts could tell her was that there was nothing wrong with her and that the baby was a perfectly healthy boy, twenty-six weeks along.

Adriana was tired of the doctors.

She went to a medicine woman. To be honest "witch" felt like a more accurate word for the strange woman who resided forty minutes outside of town in a shack tucked against one muddy bank of the Brazos River. The solitary house was creepy at best, a possible crime scene at worst. Twelve weeks ago, Adriana would never have pictured herself going to such a person. But twelve weeks ago, she wasn't twenty-six weeks pregnant.

It was her mother who suggested it. When Adriana had finally sucked it up and called her to tell her what was going on, all her mother, a born and bred local, had had to say was, "Bad luck. Better see the river woman."

It was perhaps the only valuable piece of advice her mother had ever given her. But that had yet to be seen as she'd only just knocked on the door of the "river woman."

The person who answered the door looked to be as old as the Brazos itself. She was short and round and frowning. The combination put Adriana in mind of a bullfrog.

"Yes?" the woman said, her voice surprisingly strong for her wizened appearance.

"Hello, my name is Adriana Lawrence. I have a problem I was told you might be able to help me with."

"What problem?"

Adriana almost started to tell her about the abnormal pregnancy, but she paused, remembering what her mother had said on the phone.

"Bad luck," she said instead.

The river woman nodded and let her in.

The home was as dingy and shabby inside as it was outside. It smelled like dirt and dead plants and it was certainly a change of pace from the disinfectant and bright, gleaming white of the doctor's offices and hospital rooms. The maroon threadbare couch she sat on was almost a welcome reprieve, even if Adriana still felt uncertain about being here at all.

The woman introduced herself as Cora and Adriana told her about the baby. Cora raised a hand toward Adriana's belly. "May I?"

"Yes."

The river woman reached out with both hands then, as if she were preparing to pick up something fragile.

Adriana didn't know what she was hoping for exactly, but it certainly wasn't what she got. The baby squirmed, a churning, uncomfortable twist that had its mother gasping and bowing in half. A sharp kick landed on Cora's hands and the woman jerked back, eyes wide and glued to Adriana's stomach. The force of the kick lanced through Adriana's abdomen, keeping her doubled over. She breathed through her mouth until the pain passed, then righted herself.

The baby stilled.

"What just happened?" Adriana asked.

Cora's wild gaze landed on her pale face. "You looked at the blue moon."

Adriana shook her head, not understanding. "Everyone looks at the blue moon."

Cora's gaze was heavy on her. "Not long enough for the moon to look back."

Adriana's spine stiffened.

"There is a legend. That any woman who stares at the blue moon too long will become pregnant with the moon's child."

Adriana's jaw dropped. "You can't be serious. Are you trying to tell me that the moon got me pregnant?"

"I am not telling you that at all. It is only a legend. But there is always some truth in legends."

"What else does the legend say?"

"Supposedly, blue-moon mothers give birth to demon children," said Cora, "but this is not true."

"Then what…" Adriana didn't want to ask, but she had to. "What is it?"

Cora paused, then said, "Celestial."

"It's not…It's not human?"

Cora shook her head.

Dread welled in Adriana's stomach, alongside the unnatural spawn there. It sounded crazy. And yet. What other explanation did Adriana have? Science had been stumped by it. If folklore and old wives' tales were all she had to go on, then so be it.

"What do I do?"

"You carry the child to term. It is your only option."

Adriana worried about the fabric of her shirt between her fingers. Her belly sat bulging under her hands. "Am I... am I going to be okay?"

The river woman eyed her for a long moment, something strained in her expression. Her reply was: "You know what Brazos means? The river's name?"

The question threw her, but Adriana answered. "Yes. It means "arms" in Spanish."

"That's right. This is the Río de los Brazos de Dios. And here in the "Arms of God" it will all work out."

With that small comfort Adriana went back home and waited. The expectant mother's belly grew. She felt enormous. Her feet were swollen and she waddled when she walked, back bowed to compensate for the boulder attached to her midsection.

Adriana continued to see Dr. Moorjani, who assured her with every ultrasound that the baby looked perfectly healthy. That made one of them. Dr. Moorjani started to make a lot of noises about bed rest and not straining herself and risk of hypertension.

Week fourteen of her pregnancy Adriana officially quit her jobs at the coffee shop and library and moved back in with her mother. She didn't apply for the spring semester of school because she couldn't be certain of her due date.

She sat in her mother's backyard and stared up at the moon every night. Her belly finally stopped growing. The contractions started as the sun went down. It had been only seventeen weeks since the night of the blue moon. And on this night it came again.

Its presence filled the small space, as doctors and nurses rushed around Adriana and her mother. She knew its touch like anyone who spent time dreaming did. It was nearly the shape of a man now, swathed in brilliant light, almost too bright to look at with human eyes. But then again, Adriana wasn't so sure she was even occupying her human body anymore, even though she could feel her mother's hand in hers, even though she could feel herself squinting, even though she could feel her body splitting in half. Her mind felt separate. Apart. As her eyes adjusted to the light Adriana realized it wasn't the shape of a man the moon had taken. It was that of a woman. Adriana watched as the celestial figure watched her. It was waiting patiently for the baby to be born.

It was then that Adriana understood. The moon could bear no children of her own. And so, she sought out surrogates to carry her children. It had never been Adriana's child growing inside her. It had always been the moon's.

Now the child was ready, ready to be born, and the moon was here to collect it. Adriana only had one last thing to do before she was free of them both. The pain was blinding in a way that even the light of the moon standing beside her could never match. There was so much noise around her, the doctor, her mother, the nurses, all clamoring. All except the silent, watchful moon.

Adriana cried out—screamed until she ran out of breath. When she fell silent, the moon approached, arms outstretched.

The arms of God…

Adriana reached out a hand.

But the moon reached for the child.

The clatter of tools, the voices of deliverers, the angry alarm of machines, and finally, the moment frozen in time when a child's cry never comes. It really had all just been bad luck.

Adriana's hand fell limp. Her skin drained of color, her body drained of blood.

Everything around her faded away, until only one thing remained.

The light of the moon—

—blue—

And then, nothing.

WELL BEING

By S.G. Baker

CONNIE STANDS IN THE SHOWER with her face turned upward beneath the spray the moment saltwater flows into her well, up through her pipes, out of her showerhead, down her cheek, and onto her tongue. Officials keep calling the water polluting portions of the aquifer around her town *saltwater*, but that's just a nicety. A damage-control method to mollify the public. *Saltwater* sounds better than the truth.

Because saltwater, she learns, tastes like poison.

Within the split second that the liquid hits her mouth, she gags and spits. And spits again. And again. She's stumbling backward out of the cascade and spitting all the while, terror coursing through her as she realizes that, with her well contaminated, she not only has no clean water in the house to rinse her mouth, but she just got doused with the saltwater.

An evil smell of rotten eggs mixes with the steam as she steps out of the bathtub, slipping on wet linoleum in her haste to get the door open and evade the stench. Her back wrenches a little with the jerk of her hip socket. A hiss of pain escapes her with the next spit. Globule after globule hits the floor as she limps away.

By the time she reaches the bathroom vanity, her mouth has dried out. Even then, she works up more saliva, determined not to allow even a molecule past her throat as she spits every drop into the sink.

That rotten-egg scent drifts out of the shower. Water still runs, tapping against porcelain and linoleum.

Connie gives up spitting. At this point, whatever might get into her, if anything, has already done so.

A glance in the mirror above the vanity shows she's drenched in the saltwater, her long, silvery-brown hair plastered against her skull, steam rising from her pale, freckled skin. When her head starts to spin with the unbearable odor, she pushes open a window, letting in a gust of wind that's torn across the prairie for the entirety of March.

Immediately, the sulfuric smell eases. Connie starts drying off with a towel she plans to burn later. Her hands shake as she squeezes saltwater out of her hair into the sink.

She needs to warn Kelsey not to use the faucets. But she allows herself a moment, breaths fluttering. Terror still ripples through her, because she can't confirm now, can she? She can't predict what's coming next.

Everyone knows what happened to people who drank the saltwater last week.

But also, no one knows, because all those people have disappeared or gone crazy.

One thought keeps hammering through Connie's mind.

What happens to folks who shower in it?

#   #   #

"I've seen those orphaned wells talked about in the voters' guide the past two elections." Earlier in the evening, Kelsey sits on the couch, watching the local news with a ballet flat dangling from her toe. Connie has never understood the trend of flats. But then, she doesn't have to wear business casual clothing like a middle school teacher. "You'd think they'd have done something about them by now, with all the earthquakes."

Frozen peas and carrots thump against the bottom of a saucepan as Connie shakes them free of a freezer bag. Typically, she'd have dinner cooked by now, but lately, there's been a run on the mini market. Her shift went into overtime today as she and Amit struggled to keep up with the checkout lines.

"It was a disposal well that triggered the earthquake. Not an orphaned well." Connie worked in the oil-and-gas industry before she got laid off, so she knows the difference.

Oil fields use disposal wells to store all the extra water that comes up with oil drilling, injecting the brackish liquid deeply back into the earth. Orphaned wells, on the other hand, dot the face of Texas where oil prospecting turned up nothing with a punch through the aquifer, abandoned as failures and claimed by no one.

Some have leaked saltwater over acres and acres of land. Others have simply exploded.

When Kelsey flips a hand, her gaze glued to the TV, the classroom exercises she has spread across the couch in piles of *graded, to grade*, and *come back to* slither around on the jostled couch cushion. "Whatever. The disposal wells, then."

"No, you're right that the orphaned wells are what's been a voting issue." Water gushes from the kitchen faucet as Connie tugs the sink lever toward cold. An experimental sniff reveals no scent of hydrogen sulfide gas, so she fills the saucepan. When the state survey team came in to test the groundwater, they declared her well safe. Still, she checks. "But it was a disposal well that caused the earthquake."

Over a week ago, a 5.8 magnitude earthquake jerked the mini-market floor out from under Connie's feet when it struck just nine miles northwest of town.

One moment, she was typing in a produce code for snow peas, the next, she lay sprawled on the floor. Lights flickered as overhead lamps swayed. A potted plant from the gardening-center corner tipped and crashed, splintering blue ceramic across green and white tiles. Plaster dust rained from the ceiling. Someone screamed.

Real, serious earthquakes rarely struck the Texas high plains. When they did, their causes ran down a list of likelihoods.

First, Oklahoma. Earthquakes in Oklahoma often rippled outward into the panhandle.

Second, fracking, though Connie knew fracking itself didn't cause the earthquakes. Disposal wells, where the water used for fracking got stored, began pushing back from over-pressurization.

Coming in dead last were natural earthquakes, these so small as to go unnoticed. Significant fault lines just didn't exist under the caprock.

This earthquake, according to the United States Geological Survey, was the biggest in panhandle history.

Connie hadn't known what to do. Get in a doorway? This wasn't California, and in the moment of facing an earthquake—a real one—a doorway seemed flimsy safety at best.

Unable to get up with the floor bucking beneath her, let alone reach the entrance, Connie had rolled up to crouch against her terminal, grateful for the tiny overhang of space beneath the conveyer belt. She fought not to imagine the building falling in on her and trapping her beneath piles of rubble until the shaking at last subsided.

Now Kelsey twists around on the couch to peer at Connie across the arm. Her light-brown hair hangs long and loose, fine like Connie's. Her pointed face takes more after her dad's than Connie's square one, but they share the same protruding ears. "What do you think happens to them?"

Them has become another polite moniker for what everyone wants to talk about without doing so outright.

"They said arsenic poisoning." Connie sets the saucepan on the stove and twists the knob under the burner back and forth until flames burst forth with a soft purr. She pulls thawed chicken from the fridge, ripping the cellophane packaging off. Stretchy plastic clings to her fingertips.

"I researched that." Kelsey points at Connie. "Arsenic is a slow poison that leads to cancer. Not…not…"

Not madness. Not vanishing within days of accidentally drinking contaminated groundwater.

Where some of Connie's and Kelsey's neighbors and friends have vanished to remains a mystery. Though the official statement emphasized arsenic poisoning, the gossip mill around town tells a different story. *Why* they disappeared comes from those folks who got caught on their way out.

Because no one took them. They left of their own accord.

A few days after the earth shook, families began having to restrain parents, children, siblings—young and old—as they struggled to walk out of homes, jobs, school, sports practice. Spared the fate of those who succeeded in vanishing without anyone noticing, they babbled on and on about following the salt.

In one way or another, it turns out, all of those now locked in bedrooms and kept under watch have one thing in common: they got a swallow of saltwater released into the local aquifer with the earthquake.

A sip from a water fountain. A drink from a glass of tap water. Maybe even a quick swig from a garden hose. At first, they related the salty flavor, how they hadn't thought anything of it. Municipal water tastes terrible sometimes, after all.

Now they rant and rave, clawing at walls or rocking back and forth in corners, no longer lucid enough to explain themselves, screaming for the salt.

If she gets home from work early enough, Connie hears the keening of her neighbor's kid, his unearthly, unbroken wail vibrating the afternoon air. He goes off at the same time every day. She wonders how long his family will hold out before they send him to a psychiatric hospital.

When Connie meets Kelsey's gaze, fear fills her daughter's brown eyes.

"It doesn't matter." She slices a knife through the flesh of the chicken. "Whatever happened, it's over. We're okay."

Government officials and insurance company representatives have already crawled all over town like ants on an abandoned donut, testing groundwater and surveying damage. Connie herself will be getting a payout for a massive crack down the wall of her laundry room.

Her well and those around hers got the greenlight. Though the middle school's water took a hit, the brackishness seems to have passed on. Uneven pollution of local groundwater has some of the survey team arguing with each other, Connie has heard, but all of them agree the saltwater didn't come from the disturbed disposal well.

They don't know the source, they say. Groundwater moves in mysterious ways.

"Right." Dropping her gaze, Kelsey just nods and gulps from a water bottle at her side.

Frowning, Connie finishes slicing up the chicken before laying strips in a pan of hot oil. She senses she's disappointed Kelsey with her answer. But there's nothing to do now. Natural forces impacted their community faster than anyone could have responded to the danger.

At this point, families can only wait, praying their loved ones snap out of it. Hoping the missing come back home.

Because not a single one has turned back up. Alive or dead.

#   #   #

After her saltwater shower, Connie scratches at dry, itchy skin as she limps out of her bedroom, dressed in a blue t-shirt and faded denim jeans and looking for her shoes. She needs to find an uncontaminated shower to wash the saltwater off. She needs to warn Kelsey about the pollution. She needs to burn these clothes as soon as she's clean.

But Kelsey isn't on the couch where Connie left her to get her shower. A guy on the TV behind a beige news station desk reports on the strange case plaguing the Texas town of Barranca. *"Officials continue to monitor the situation. Barranca's mayor has requested psychiatric help for those affected by the groundwater, prompting speculation that…"*

Connie snorts at the report. Mayor Hernandez requested official psych evals for the victims right away, but the Railroad Commission, in charge of monitoring and managing oil-and-gas-related wells, has tied up the request in arguments of financial responsibility.

"Kelsey?"

Connie slips her phone from her pocket and shoots texts off to her neighbors. *Saltwater in my well. Don't drink your water.*

"Kels?"

As she locates her shoes under the coffee table where she kicked them off while she and Kelsey ate dinner, Connie keeps listening for the sound of a toilet flushing or a door closing. Nothing reaches her. The quiet of the house lacks that held-breath pregnancy of another occupant.

It feels empty.

Connie sits in the armchair and laces up her shoes, dialing Kelsey's number from memory when she's done. Kelsey's phone lying on the couch arm lights up. Connie ends the call, staring as the screen goes dark.

It's fine, it's fine. Maybe she just went for a walk and left her phone for a little peace.

But now that she looks, Connie notes the scattering of Kelsey's graded papers. How her neat piles have slid into each other, as if jostled when she got up, uncaring.

Connie scratches her arm. "Kelsey!"

A creak sounds from the laundry room, like the back door has just opened.

Relief trickles through Connie. That must be Kelsey. As she stands, she grabs Kelsey's water bottle from the end table. At least she can rinse out her mouth. Taking a big swig and swishing the water around, she steps into the laundry room.

As she registers the back door hanging open, no Kelsey in sight, the horrible rancid flavor of saltwater coats her tongue.

Connie spits and spits and spits again, stamping her feet as a tiny scream of terror erupts from her. No point in screaming for real. Kelsey won't hear her.

Kelsey was drinking the saltwater.

Kelsey is gone.

\#   \#   \#

Deputy Brent Hibbetts does little to find Kelsey beyond checking through Connie's house and walking around her yard with a flashlight. When she holds up the bottle and tells him what's inside, he backs away as if she's wielding a live rattler.

"I have to take that." Hibbetts, with his crew cut and big stance—hands on his hips, always leaning forward a bit—looks like he'd rather walk barefoot through a bed of sharp goathead weeds than accept that bottle. He pulls on a latex glove, as if that will somehow protect him where a plastic barrier wouldn't. "Why do you even have this?"

"Kelsey…" Connie hands the bottle over and tugs at her fingers. "I think she was drinking it."

Hibbetts's expression turns horrified. "Why?"

"I don't know." But Connie can guess.

Maybe Kelsey figured that people who screamed about following the salt needed more of the saltwater. Without it, they began to think of nothing else. If she accidentally drank some at the school and saw what happened to people afterward, she might've decided to risk drinking more to satiate her desire. So she wouldn't disappear.

"What do you think happens to them?"

Kelsey's question echoes through Connie's mind. Did she know? Did she realize drinking the saltwater had begun to satisfy her need less and less? Did she suspect she would leave soon?

Plastic crinkles and liquid sloshes as Hibbets drops the mostly empty bottle into a plastic evidence bag. "You'll have to vacate the premises while your water gets tested for biohazards." He glances around Connie's cramped living room. "Do you have somewhere to go?"

As he seals the bag up, Connie notes how the water appears…cloudy. If memories of earthquakes and keening children hadn't distracted her, she would've recognized the saltwater earlier. She shrugs. "A motel."

Though Connie finds his search-and-rescue efforts wanting, she and Hibbetts share a look. One that says they both know the nearest motel lies in the next town an hour away. With nowhere to stay in Barranca, she's screwed.

"If Kelsey doesn't turn up in the morning, come by the station to fill out a missing person report." Hibbetts straightens, back in control with the saltwater safely contained. "And you'll get an update on the well-water test."

He's leaving. He's handing Connie a business card with a case number penned on the back. He's stepping out the door into the night, having accomplished nothing.

Connie follows him out onto the porch. "Has anyone been found yet?"

Hibbetts pauses, his big shoulders rising and falling with a deep breath. "No."

In that moment, he's not a law enforcement officer talking to a concerned citizen. They're community members, struck by the same tragedy, unable to affect any change. Helpless to solve a problem no one understands.

A clatter rises from the trailer house next door as the porch light flicks on. Connie's neighbors, the Meltons, set several suitcases and duffels outside, stationing two of their young children near the bags. Ashley follows, helping Leo grip a writhing third child in his arms. Their boy holds his mouth wide, wide open, like a baby bird begging for a worm, as he pushes himself away from Leo's chest.

Hair on the back of Connie's neck rises. After drinking the saltwater while playing afterschool baseball, this boy now sends up cries that split the air every afternoon. He looks like he's still screaming, just at a pitch no one can hear.

As a unit, the family aims for the car in their gravel driveway, with Ashley directing the children to collect bags and fussing around Leo and the boy. Spotting Connie and Hibbetts on the porch, she takes a step closer. "Thanks for the text about the water."

"Is your well affected, too, Mrs. Melton?" Hibbetts shifts his weight and his interest toward the neighbors, ready to deal with the next problem.

"It smells bad. We're going out of town until we can get it fixed." Ashley glances back at the car, hollering for the kids to put their bags in the trunk and themselves in the back seat.

"That's for the best."

Connie watches the wide-mouthed boy disappear into the cab as Leo buckles him in.

With Kelsey gone, there's no one to stop her from vanishing, too. A black future opens up before her.

Missing or mad.

Porch slats creak as Hibbets steps off and heads toward his cruiser parked next to Kelsey's powder-blue car. "I'll check in on the Popes on the other side."

I tasted the saltwater, almost exits Connie's mouth. *It poured over me. Lock me up before I disappear forever. At least I'll still be alive, even if I'm insane.*

But where do people who yearn for the salt go? Who can find them but those also contaminated?

Connie seals her lips shut and steps back inside, the weight of her decision like a rock in her chest.

#   #   #

A full moon reflects abundant light across an unfamiliar empty field, illuminating the distant dip of a draw, where water has cut through the caprock but only flows during the occasional rainstorm. Everything around Connie—from tall prairie grass fronds to bushy yucca leaves to sprawls of prickly pear to thorny mesquite trees dotting the crumbled ridge above the draw—glitters blue.

But before her, a round pool of water glows bluest of all.

Relaxed hands resting on her thighs, knees almost touching the water, Connie kneels at the pool's edge like a penitent. A worshiper. A disciple to salt.

When she went to bed after Hibbets left, she had the forethought to keep her shoes on. No yearning for saltwater burned on her tongue as she rested atop her comforter, however, letting her imagine she might not wander off after all. Only the dry itch all over her body dug at her. No amount of hydrocortisone cream soothed her skin.

Connie didn't think she would ever sleep again.

As she lay there, a knife kept piercing her heart every time she remembered Kelsey's absence. Her daughter didn't scroll her phone in the next bedroom. Didn't take her sleeping pill so she wouldn't toss and turn with anxiety. Didn't dream of the children at school who looked up to her.

Her baby was gone.

Connie's loss of Kelsey's father didn't even begin to compare. He'd died, and with his death, Connie could do nothing more for him. All the doctor visits and specialist appointments and necessary care and pill reminders ended. But Kelsey going missing—the not knowing her fate—prompts action. Effort. Sacrifice.

Full moon light poured through her bedroom window, which she had only to turn her head on her pillow to gaze through, hoping to see Kelsey's form out there on the prairie. *Worm moon*, Connie thought. She'd heard the March full moon signals the arrival of worms crawling up out of the earth.

When at last she did drift off, she fell asleep wishing to submerge herself in saltwater. Anything to stop the maddening itch.

Right now, under the flood of moonlight brightening the entire field, Connie feels like a worm herself. Scratches mar the dry, flaking skin of her bare arms, a collection of crisscross lacerations from walking through mesquite tree branches—apparently with no heed to their inch-long thorns—and parallel marks from her own fingernails. A few of the cuts ooze sluggish blood.

Connie remembers nothing about the trek to this place. She doesn't even know where here is. But she managed to reach this field in one night, going by the moon's enduring fullness. Still, the satellite's size has begun to increase and its shape to yellow, a gold coin sinking toward the horizon, distorted by atmosphere.

Morning will arrive soon.

Not quite circular, the pool at Connie's knees leads down and down and down, natural sides disappearing into a bundle of blue light shining up from deep below.

Unlike typical orphaned wells, this one does not overflow with pressurized water awaiting release. Its still surface sits level within a ring of pale, sparkling gypsum chunks, these perhaps pushed free during the recent earthquake. Also unlike most orphaned wells, this one spans several yards in diameter rather than mere inches.

A big metal well plug lies nearby, rolled a little distance from the pool and resting on two enormous pressure wheels set in its front. A rusted chain looped between the two prevents the wheels from turning, but that makes no difference when the entire conical cap has snapped off at the base.

Connie gets the impression that this orphaned well, maybe lost to ancient peoples with the vagaries of invasion and colonization, became covered up a second time with intent. Whoever placed that cap—a long, long time ago, judging by the model—punched into this well looking for oil and found only horror.

They meant for no one to ever drink the water here again and left no record of its location for a reason.

This impression has a lot to do with the bodies.

Below, people float suspended in the liquid at varying levels, neither rising nor sinking, like flies trapped in amber. Wives and dads Connie has chatted with at work close to the top. Her neighbor, who waves when she passes, among a cluster in the middle. Her husband's gaming buddy off to the side, pointed downward as if he dived as far as he could. Only a foot or so separates the soles of his shoes from the surface.

Some hang face down, recognizable only by clothes and hair. Many stare at Connie with wide-open eyes. But none blink like Kelsey does where she floats beneath them all, gazing up at her.

Connie recognizes the inherent ritual here at once. Devotees exposed to the saltwater as much as possible before attempting a pilgrimage to the depths. Wills clashing between contaminated devotee and the demanding call of a well that resists anyone insufficiently prepared with too little saltwater.

Queasiness snakes through her stomach. She scratches her arm until more blood flows.

Below, Kelsey blinks. Slow, languid. Her lips move, but Connie can't guess at her intended message.

A fingertip dipped into the liquid reveals a certain thick viscosity—a clingy buoyancy that resists both Connie's intrusion and departure.

At just that bare touch, electricity zings over every inch of her fiery skin. Like calling to like. This well knows her. Recognizes the salt clinging to her in pale, peeling flakes. If Connie dips herself in, her agonized itching will end.

If she drowns herself in the saltwater, ecstasy—pure and eternal—will follow.

Connie catches her palms against the chalky gypsum chunks ringing the well, just stopping herself from diving in. Face close enough for her breath to ripple the surface, she hangs there, her arm muscles straining against the yearning that brought her to this shrine.

She's going in. She's going in. She knows she's going in. When is just a matter of minutes. Seconds. Her next heartbeat.

If she does, she and Kelsey will meet the same fate. Suspended forever in an orphaned well as more and more unwitting devotees topple in, trapped near the surface because of a mere mouthful of polluted water. Connie perhaps deepest of all for having showered in the stuff. But stuck there all the same until they both stop blinking.

Unless she completes the ritual.

In the millisecond that the thought crosses her mind, Connie loses the fight against herself and plunges face-first into the well.

Saltwater parts around her, sliding over her skin and through her clothes as silkily as pure spring water. Saltwater clings to her, molding itself to her form like cellophane. Saltwater embraces her, holding her back barely at all, a mere formality before giving in.

Connie only has eyes for Kelsey. And below her, that cold blue light.

She has the presence of mind to push off the ledge surrounding the pool with her toes, hating the sensation of swimming in shoes. Cloth brushes her hands as she grabs the shoulders or the legs of neighbors and friends she swims past, using body parts to pull herself deeper. Bubbles rise as if through gel as she releases her air, the faster to sink.

A gap between the lowest body and Kelsey opens up. Drinking all that saltwater got her daughter so far down. Much deeper than the rest.

Only there, in that small but enormous gap, does panic lance through Connie. She's in the well, there's no going back, she will die here. If she can't sink all the way down to Kelsey, she will have accomplished nothing at all.

In that space, close, so close now, Kelsey blinks. Long hair halos around her, limned in blue light. Her lips part, but no bubbles rush out. Saltwater has permeated her down to her lungs.

Her hand opens, reaching.

Connie closes her fingers on Kelsey's.

With no time for reunion, Connie slingshots herself past Kelsey, pulling hard on Kelsey's arm to fling her upward. Doing so forces her even farther down, twisting her around to sink backward toward the overbright depths.

She hopes she put enough force behind the yank. That she didn't hold back even a bit.

She hopes the well will accept a little cheating.

Even though Connie watches Kelsey's sluggish progress upward until she breaks the surface, blue, blue, blue rises around her, filling the edges of her vision.

If she's right, with the well satisfied, the call of the salt will end. Kelsey will get to live. Everyone will forget the saltwater and, perhaps, the pool's location. Maybe another injection-site earthquake will bury this incomprehensible shrine altogether.

At least for now.

Connie's world goes white, blotting out her view of Kelsey climbing out of the well. Of her arm plunging back in, fingers outstretched toward Connie. Always needing her. Always reaching for her mother.

With her last shred of air, a triumphant scream rips out of Connie. She's won the race to the bottom. A brilliant electric charge lights up her mind, the promise of euphoria fulfilled, wave after wave rolling through her.

On her next and final gasp, her lungs fill with salt and salt and salt and salt.

BIOS

Jacklyn Baker is a Texas transplant living in Minnesota who has always had an obsession with monsters and what they mean. She learned the craft of writing via the SMU Writers' Path and has since worked on various projects, ranging from short stories to comic books. When not writing, she can be found acting in cheesy movies via Saint Euphoria Pictures. You can find her at jacklynbaker.com.

S.G. Baker is a writer and editor who has authored climate fiction, fantasy, thriller, and horror short stories in *Freelancer*, *The Legacy: Weird Stories and Dark Tales*, *Little Blue Marble: Warmer Worlds*, and *Road Kill: Texas Horror by Texas Writers*. Find more from her at summergbaker.com.

Madison Estes is the editor of *Road Kill Vol. 6* and is currently working on her debut short story collection. When she's not playing JRPGs or escape room games, she's writing, drawing or running a horrortube channel.

Jess Hagemann's recent work has appeared or is forthcoming in the *San Antonio Current*, *Three Seasons of Winter*, and *Last Girls Club*, among others. Her debut novel *Headcheese* (2018) won an IPPY Award in Horror. *Paste Magazine* named her sophomore novel *Mother-Eating*, which marries Marie Antoinette and cults, one of the "Most-Anticipated Horror Books of 2025." Jess received her MFA from the Jack Kerouac School, and has been awarded a teaching fellowship at McNeese State University as well as a writing residency at Dear Butte. She lives in Austin. More at jesshagemann.com.

R. J. Joseph is an award winning, Shirley Jackson and Stoker Award™ nominated Texas based writer/speaker/editor. Her creative and academic work examines the intersections of race, gender, and class in the horror genre and popular culture. She has most recently been at work with Raw Dog Screaming Press on their new novella line, Selected Papers from the

Consortium for the Study of Anomalous Phenomena. She occasionally peeks out on various social media platforms from behind @rjacksonjoseph or at rhondajacksonjoseph.com.

Kathleen Kent is a New York Times bestselling author of historical fiction and an Edgar Award Nominee for her contemporary crime trilogy, *The Dime, The Burn* and *The Pledge.* Her newest novel, *Black Wolf*, an international spy thriller, has received glowing reviews in both the US and the UK. She has written short stories and essays for *D Magazine, Texas Monthly* and LitHub, and has been published in several crime anthologies. In March 2020 she was inducted into the Texas Institute of Letters for her contribution to Texas literature.

Jae Mazer is a Canadian who was born in Victoria, British Columbia, and grew up in the prairies of Northern Alberta. After spending the majority of her life battling sasquatches in the Great White North, she migrated south to Texas to have a go at the armadillos. She is a connoisseur and creator of gothic horror, splatterfolk, splatter westerns, and folk horror. She's degreed, won awards, been in anthologies, owns a couple of breweries, has chameleon hair and lots of skin ink, and enjoys mustard and alcohol.

Emma E. Murray writes horror and dark speculative fiction. Her work includes *Crushing Snails, The Drowning Machine and Other Obsessions, Shoot Me in the Face on a Beautiful Day,* and *When the Devil.* When she isn't writing, she's either reading or playing pretend with her daughter. She is represented by Clara Chuiton of The Rights Factory.

Lauren Oertel is a writer, editor, workshop facilitator, and community organizer based in Austin, Texas. She is the coauthor of the collaborative book, *Inside Out: A Texas Prisons Poetry Story*, and her debut full-length poetry collection, *Scars & Other Luxuries*, is forthcoming in 2026.

L.H. Phillips is a retired molecular biologist with a life-long love of speculative fiction. Her previous stories have appeared in *Aphelion, The*

Nameless Songs of Zadok Allen, *Road Kill vol. 9*, *Mysterion*, *Behind the Revolving Door*, and *Starship Blunder 2*. She lives in San Antonio, TX with her husband and cat.

Iphigenia Strangeworth became a horror author because she couldn't afford therapy. When she isn't writing, she can be found reading, drawing, embroidering, or lecturing her uninterested family members about shipwrecks.

A Native Texan of Mexican-American heritage, **Carmen Gray** is a retired Dual Language teacher in Austin and a writer whose work appears in multiple volumes of *Road Kill: Texas Horror by Texas Writers* and in several anthologies published by Castle Bridge Media. She has two novels in progress and poetry in various publications. A freelance writer and editor for multiple publications, she is also a member of The Writers League of Texas, a Chateau d'Orquevaux Writing Residency awardee, recipient of a Landmarks of American History and Culture grant and has been a moderator at the Texas Book Festival. When she's not with her family, she teaches yoga, wanders the streets of foreign cities, and reads tarot alongside her animal familiars.

CASTLE BRIDGE MEDIA RECOMMENDS...

If you liked this book, you might also enjoy reading the following titles from Castle Bridge Media available on Amazon or by order at your favorite book store:

The 23rd Hero
By Rebecca Anne Nguyen

ANIMAL CHARMER
By Rain Nox
Animal Charmer
Magic & Melody

Austinites
By In Churl Yo

Bloodsucker City
By Jim Towns

SOUL CATCHER
By Don Sawyer
The Burning Gem
The Tunnels of Buda

THE CASTLE OF HORROR ANTHOLOGY SERIES
Volume 1
Volume 2: Holiday Horrors
Volume 3: Scary Summer
   Stories
Volume 4: Women Running
   From Houses
Volume 5: Thinly Veiled:
   The 70s
Volume 6: Femme Fatales*
Volume 7: Love Gone Wrong
Volume 8: Thinly Veiled:
   The 80s
Volume 9: Young Adult
Volume 10: Thinly Veiled:
   Saturday Mournings
Volume 11: Revenge
Volume 12: Ripped From
   The Headlines
Edited By Jason Henderson
and In Churl Yo
*Edited By P.J. Hoover

Child of Dark Water
By E.G. Rand

Castle of Horror Podcast
Book of Great Horror:
Our Favorites, Top Tens
and Bizarre Pleasures
Edited By Jason Henderson

Cherry Dark
By R.L. Wilburn

Dream State
By Martin Ott

Dominic
By Lee Guzman

FRENCH DECEPTION
By Janice Nagourney
A Forgery in Paris
A Forgery in Lyon
A Forgery in Marseille

FuturePast Sci-Fi Anthology
Edited by In Churl Yo

GLAZIER'S GAP
Ghosts of the Forbidden
By Leanna Renee Hieber

Hellfall
By Jay Gould

Isonation
By In Churl Yo

JAYU CITY CHRONICLES
By Chris M. Arnone
The Hermes Protocol
Necropolis Alpha

Junk Film: Why Bad
Movies Matter
By Katharine Coldiron

Nightwalkers:
Gothic Horror Movies
By Bruce Lanier Wright

MID-LIFE CRISIS THRILLERS
18 Miles From Town
By Jason Henderson
Lost Angel
By Sam Knight

Ties That Kill
By Deven Greene

THE PATH
By David Bowles
The Blue-Spangled Blue
The Deepest Green

Strange Shape of Love
By Herta Feely

SURF MYSTIC
By Peyton Douglas
Night of the Book Man
Dark of the Curl

The Thing That Happened
When We Were Little
By Caroline Kelly Franklin

Tick Town
By Christopher A. Micklos

Yesterday's Tomorrows:
The Golden Age of
Science Fiction Movies
By Bruce Lanier Wright

Please remember to leave us your reviews on Amazon and Goodreads!

THANK YOU FOR SUPPORTING INDEPENDENT PUBLISHERS AND AUTHORS!
castlebridgemedia.com